∽ THE ∽
BREAKUP BIBLE

A NOVEL BY
MELISSA KANTOR

HYPERION

NEW YORK

Printed in the United States of America

First Edition
10 9 8 7 6 5 4 3 2
Library of Congress Cataloging-in-Publication Data on file.
ISBN-13:978-0-7868-0962-2
ISBN-10:0-7868-0962-0
Reinforced binding
Designed by Elizabeth H. Clark
Visit www.hyperionteens.com

To Bernie Kaplan and Helen Perelman

PART ONE
The End
♥ ♥

ONE

· · ·

I AM TRYING TO BREAK YOUR HEART

IN NINETEENTH-CENTURY NOVELS, characters die of heartbreak. Literally. A girl gets dumped, and she's so grief-stricken she suffers a "brain fever," or goes wandering out on the moors, and the next thing you know, the whole town is hovering by her bedside while a servant gallops on a desperate midnight ride to fetch the doctor. Only, before you can say *Bring on the leeches!* the guilt-ridden rake who abandoned our heroine is strewing rose petals on her grave and begging God to *Please, take me, too* because his ex is dead, dead, *dead.*

According to Mrs. Hamilton, my English teacher, this is known as a "convention." After writing CONVEN-TION on the blackboard, she gave us a lecture explaining that conventions are things we accept when they happen in books and movies even though they never happen in real life. Then she asked us to think of some modern conventions, like how characters on soap operas get amnesia constantly, and in teen movies the only thing an ugly girl needs to be pretty is contact lenses and a new haircut, when in real life if an ugly girl gets contact lenses and a new haircut, she's just an ugly girl with contact lenses and a new haircut.

But when Max told me that he'd "been thinking about it a lot lately" and had "decided it would be better if we were just friends," it occurred to me that dying of a broken heart might not be a convention. I unbuckled my seat belt, slid out of his car, and shut the door. As the freezing February air slapped my cheeks, I thought, *That's the last time I'm going to get out of Max's car.* And right after that I thought, *I'm never going to kiss Max again.* And then I thought, *Max isn't my boyfriend anymore.* And that's when I knew I was going to be sick. I got inside my house with barely enough time to drop my bag and make it to the upstairs bathroom before I hurled. And then I spent about an hour lying on the cold tile floor trying to get up the strength to walk from the bathroom to my room, which is a distance of roughly ten feet. And when I finally *did* manage to make it to my room, I just got into bed without taking off my clothes or anything. Right before I fell asleep, I decided that whoever made the brilliant so-called medical decision that death by heartbreak was only a "convention" of nineteenth-century literature clearly never had her heart broken.

Because if anything can make death feel like a truly desirable alternative, it's getting dumped.

♥ ♥ ♥

I'd had an insane crush on Max Brown since I first joined the *Hillsdale High Spectator* as a lowly freshman reporter. By this fall, when I was a junior and the newly appointed managing editor of the paper, and Max was a senior and editor in chief, I liked him so much I could hardly read in his presence (which, as you can imagine, made editing the paper something of a challenge). But even though we were constantly engaging in flirty banter, and he was forever saying stuff to me like, "Jennifer, you know I'd be lost without you," nothing ever *happened*.

Until.

Until the third Saturday in September, when Jeremy Peterson chose to honor the trust his parents had placed in him by throwing an enormous kegger at his house while they went out of town for the weekend.

Jeremy Peterson and Max are really good friends, so there was zero doubt Max would be in attendance (and, by extension, zero doubt *I'd* be there). Arriving fashionably late, my friends Clara and Martha and I passed Max's Mini Cooper parked in the driveway. Both of them gave me significant looks as we walked by the car, but none of us said a word; good secret agents know better than to discuss a mission in progress.

The three of us hung out in the kitchen for a while drinking beers, and then I said I was going to go to the bathroom, which we all knew was a lie; clearly I was going to look for Max. We had a positive car ID. He was in the house. The only question that remained was: where?

I got my answer walking down the hallway that ran past the den. There he was, sitting on the Petersons' modular sofa talking to Jeremy and two other seniors, Michael Roach and Greg Cobb. Just as I walked by, Max turned his head toward the open door and brushed the hair out of his eyes. And then he saw me. And I saw him see me, and he saw me see him see me, and it was like all those months and years of flirting suddenly exploded or something. I swear to God you could have powered all of Westchester County on the look that passed between us.

Max raised an eyebrow at me and gestured to the empty spot on the sofa next to him, and I went over and sat down without either of us saying a word. Then I sat there listening to him and the three other coolest guys in the senior class argue about whether Franz Ferdinand or Wilco is the band that's more likely to leave an enduring musical legacy. (At first I didn't actually realize they were bands—I thought they were people, and that Wilco was a guy who went by a single name, like Madonna or Beyoncé.)

During a particularly heated exchange between Jeremy and Michael, Max turned to me.

"Do you know these bands?" Max is a lot taller than I am, but the couch was the kind you sink way down into and we were both leaning back, almost reclining, so his mouth was only an inch or two away from my ear.

Normally I would have tried to come up with some witty way to avoid admitting I hadn't even realized they *were* bands, but there was nothing normal about this night. So I just said, "No."

Max stood up. "Hey, Jeremy, you got any Wilco in your room?"

Jeremy was leaning forward, telling Michael he was starting to sound like a guy who listens to smooth jazz. He looked over at Max, gave him a quizzical scowl and said, "Is the Pope Catholic?" before turning back to Michael.

Max reached his hand down to me. "Come on," he said. His hand was warm, and when I stood up, he intertwined his fingers with mine.

He took me up a narrow flight of dark stairs. Without saying a word, he crossed the hall and entered a room, pulling me in behind him before closing the door. Then he turned on a small desk lamp and ran his fingers down a stack of precariously balanced CDs.

"God, what a loser," he muttered, pausing at one of them and laughing a little to himself. I'd barely had time to look around Jeremy's room and take in the unmade bed, the open closet with clothes on the floor, the poster over the desk from an antiwar protest, when Max popped a disc into the CD player and turned off the lamp. Before my eyes had adjusted to the darkness, I could feel him standing next to me.

"Like it?" he asked.

My heart was pounding. It took me a minute to focus on the music, an almost atonal series of notes played by different instruments.

"Too early to tell," I answered. "Give me a second."

"Sure," he said. He'd taken my hand again, and now he took the other one. We stood there for a long moment, neither of us moving. "Well?" he asked finally.

A man with a husky voice was singing. I couldn't make out the lyrics, but I liked his voice, the way the instruments seemed to find and hold a melody around it.

I could see Max now in the dim light of the digital display. "Yeah," I said. "I like it."

He leaned down so slowly I could barely tell he was

moving. "I'm glad," he whispered. And then we were kissing, and I was thinking about how amazing it felt to be kissing him and how soft his lips were and how perfect it was to wrap my arms around his waist and then to run my fingers through his dark, silky hair.

But you know what I *should have* been thinking about? I should have been thinking about the girls in those novels. Because if I'd thought a little more about them and a little less about Max's hair and lips and how it felt when he put his hands on my face and said about our kiss, "I've been wanting to do that since I met you," then maybe I wouldn't be thinking about them now, five months later, having just been informed by the love of my life that we'll be better off as friends.

Maybe then I wouldn't be thinking that I, like them, could actually die of heartache.

TWO

· · ·

DEATH IS NOT AN OPTION

WHEN I WOKE UP, I had no memory of getting from the bathroom to my bed. My shoes and my jacket were still on, but the light wasn't. I lay in the dark listening to see if anyone was home, but the house was silent. On Fridays my brother has a late hockey practice and my mom meets with her book club. Neither of them was going to be home until late. *I'm all alone,* I thought. *I'm all alone and I wish I were dead.*

It wasn't like I couldn't have called my mom and told her I had an emergency and needed her to stop talking about *War and Peace* or *The Brothers Karamazov* and come home tout de suite to minister to her daughter, who might very possibly be on the verge of death. But my mother's book group is made up of her and all these other divorced women who, not to put too fine a point on it, hate men. One time when the book club was meeting at our house and I was waiting for Max to pick me up, my mom's best friend, Donna, actually uttered the sentence, "Do not believe a word he says to you, Jennifer." I mean, I feel bad for Donna and all, what with her husband having left her for his administrative assistant (which, let's face it, is not only painful in and of itself but is made even worse by the fact that you're reduced to being a bargain-basement cliché for the rest of your life). Yet you'd think a woman who runs her own successful real estate business could differentiate between one bad apple and *every single piece of fruit that exists on the face of the earth*. Given the company my mom was keeping this evening, I didn't need her taking my call and then explaining to everyone why she couldn't stay for the meeting. A bunch of bitter divorcées being all, *See what happens when you trust a man?* was not exactly the kind of support I was looking for.

To be fair, my mom's not as bad as Donna. But she's not exactly "Rah, rah, sis boom bah, *yeaaa, Men!*" either, what with my dad having left her five years ago. If you ask me, the fact that he realized he was *gay* and left her for *another man* makes his leaving her about as different as night and day from Donna's husband leaving her for his twenty-five-year-old (female) coworker, but somehow my mom isn't comforted by subtle distinctions like sexual orientation. She and my dad get along okay and everything, but she kind of gave Max the evil eye every time he came to pick me up, as if instead of belonging to a different gender, he belonged to a different (and highly untrustworthy) species.

So I called Clara. I would have called Martha, too, but tonight was the cast party for *Othello*, which she did costumes for. Martha's such a good friend that she would actually have bagged the party for me. But for months now she's had a mad crush on Todd Kincaid, the senior who played Othello, and the potent cocktail of nostalgia and euphoria that is a cast party seemed guaranteed to inspire Todd's confession of true love. No way was I going to let my heartbreak stand in the way of Todd and Martha getting together. Not to sound superficial or anything, but they'll be the world's hottest couple. Martha's beautiful. She's tiny with bright blue eyes, and pale, pale skin. Todd's great looking, too, but her total opposite—he's got very black skin and he's tall and broad shouldered.

Together they'll look like a Benetton ad.

Todd is the articles editor of the *Spectator*, and before Max dumped me, Martha and I had come up with all kinds of plans for how when Todd finally asked her out, the four of us would go on double dates and share a limo for the prom and stuff.

Thinking about prom, I actually groaned out loud.

♥ ♥ ♥

Luckily, Clara only lives five minutes away, and since she knows our alarm code, I didn't even have to get out of bed to let her in. It was like one second I was dialing her number and the next I was bawling all over her turtle-neck.

"I can't believe he *broke up* with you." I'd finally stopped bawling into her shoulder, and now we were just sitting next to each other on my bed. "He's *such* a jerk. How could he just *break up* with you like that?"

"Will you stop *saying* it already?" I said.

She put her arm around me. "Sorry," she said. "I'm just in shock."

I nodded and wiped my nose on my T-shirt. "What am I going to *do*?" Clara got the box of tissues off my night table and handed me one. I blew my nose into it. "I just don't get how you can love someone one second and then not love that person anymore." The words I was saying only made me cry harder. "I just don't get it." The *get it* part of my sentence came out pretty garbled because I'd started to bawl again, but Clara understood. No matter how fast one of us is talking—even if it involves a mouthful of food—the other one can always understand what she's saying.

"What am I going to do?" I repeated, pressing the heels of my hands against my eyes. "How am I going to face school?" Just saying the word "school" was chilling. I lay down in a fetal position and pulled the covers up to my ear. When that didn't help, I pulled them over my head.

Clara patted my face through the comforter. "Don't think about school yet," she said.

But now that I'd uttered the word, I couldn't *not* think about it. Ever since Max and I had started going out, I'd felt about school the way I had when I was a little kid—can't wait to get there, never want to leave. Every second felt supercharged; just walking from science to history, something exciting and wonderful could happen.

♥ ♥ ♥

The Monday after we first hooked up at Jeremy's party, my cell rang while I was on my way to second period. I didn't recognize the number, but I answered it.

"Hello?"

"Turn around," said Max, his voice calm and sexy. I turned around, and there he was. It was like a scene from a movie. People were swarming past us, running to get to class, and we just stood there, not moving, looking at each other from a distance of about twenty feet. He was wearing a flannel shirt over a white T-shirt and a worn pair of Levi's, which I think might be the sexiest thing a guy can wear since it's so totally mellow. I know some girls like it when guys worry about their clothes, but I don't (and this has nothing to do with my dad being gay because contrary to popular stereotypes, not all gay men dress like they're in an Abercrombie ad).

We kept our phones pressed to our ears.

"Hey," he said into his.

"Hey," I said into mine.

"I had a great time Saturday night."

"Me too."

"I thought about you all day Sunday." Far away as we were, I could see him smiling, and I smiled back.

"You don't say," I said. I neglected to mention that I'd spent all of Sunday wondering if he'd call, wondering if it meant anything that he hadn't called, didn't tell him I'd finally decided ours had just been a one-night thing.

"Oh, but I *do* say."

"And what'd you think about when you were thinking about me?" The crowd was thinning out, but we still didn't make a move toward each other.

Still smiling, he shook his head. "I'll never tell."

15

"Hmm . . ." I drew the word out like a purr. Then I said, "I'll take that as a compliment."

"Do that," he said. By now the hallway was almost totally empty, just a few last-minute stragglers racing to make it to class before the bell. I knew I was going to be late to history, but I didn't care. Max flipped his phone shut and said to me (the real me, not the phone me), "I'll see you at the *Spectator* meeting." His voice was just slightly louder than it had been on the phone. It was as if he had known exactly how far apart we could stand without needing to shout to be heard.

I flipped my phone shut. "See ya," I called. As I walked away, Max whistled. I forced myself not to look back at him.

♥ ♥ ♥

"Oh, God, I'm sorry," said Clara, thinking my fresh round of sobbing had been brought on by whatever she must have said while I was remembering my conversation with Max.

"No, no," I said. "It's not that." But between the comforter and the crying, even Clara couldn't understand me. Finally she eased the covers off my face.

"Look, maybe there'll be a snow day," she said. "Maybe we won't even *have* school on Monday."

Instead of making me feel better, the words

"snow day" filled me with dread. "No," I moaned.

"At least you wouldn't have to see him, right?" said Clara.

With Clara staring at me, I couldn't admit the truth, which was that I *wanted* to see Max. Clara isn't exactly tall, and with her spiky blond hair, wire-rimmed glasses, and perfect, pixie face, she looks more like a brainy Tinker Bell than Attila the Hun. But she is without a doubt the strongest person I know. She had a boyfriend at camp this summer (they were both CITs), and the day before camp ended, he dumped her just so he could spend the bus ride home making out with some other girl. Clara was in shock—he'd told her he loved her! After they broke up they didn't talk again until October, when he called her and was all, *So do you still think about me? Because I still think about you, and I think we should get back together.* Clara listened to him say he missed her and that he'd made an awful mistake and blah, blah, blah, and when he was done she just said, "Never call me again!" and hung up the phone. I couldn't *believe* it. When she told me the story I said, *Well, maybe he's really sorry. Do you think you should give him another chance?* And she said, *He had his chance. And he used it to be a total ass.*

Which, objectively, you can't really argue with.

I rolled over onto my stomach and buried my head

in the pillow. No way would Clara "Never Call Me Again" Jaffe understand that the only thing getting me through the weekend was the knowledge that I was going to see Max on Monday, and that maybe sometime between now and then he'd realize what a terrible mistake he'd made. Because if that happened, you were definitely *not* going to be hearing the words "Never call me again" emerge from my mouth.

"I have to pee," I said.

While I was washing my hands, I examined myself in the mirror. On a good day, the most you could say about my hair—which is straight and brown and medium length—is that it's inoffensive. Right now, however, it looked like I was overdue for an extreme makeover. And my face, generally fairly forgettable, resembled something a close-up of which might open a horror movie: *Scientist: "And zis iz vhat ve discovered ven ve dug up ze svamp." (He pulls a sheet off the examining table, revealing a waterlogged head. The assembled crowd gasps with horror and revulsion.)*

Max used to tell me I was sexy. We'd be fooling around or even talking about something totally *unsexy*, like whether we wanted a headline to have punctuation or not, and suddenly he'd look at me, really *look* at me, and go, "God, you're sexy."

Maybe if you're one of those girls who's always

hearing that from guys, it's not that big a deal. Like maybe when someone tells Jessica Rabassa (this total supermodel-type senior who wears black all the time, has had about fifty boyfriends, and can barely be bothered to put out her cigarette when it's time to go to class) that she's sexy, she's just like, "Yeah, and . . . ?"

But no one had ever said that to me before Max.

And thinking about how it used to make me feel when he said it—how I both didn't believe him and, at the same time, how his saying it made me feel sexy so I kind of couldn't *not* believe him—and thinking about how he wasn't ever going to say it to me again, made me feel even worse than I'd felt when I was just staring at myself in the mirror and thinking I looked like total crap.

I must have been in the bathroom longer than I'd realized because there was a knock on the door.

"Jenny, are you okay?" It was Clara.

I shook my head, but then I realized she couldn't see me, so I just said, "No." It came out more like a squeak than a word, since I'd started crying again.

Slowly the door opened. "Do you want me to make you a fruit smoothie?" Clara makes unbelievable fruit smoothies (the secret ingredient is lemon juice). But the thought of consuming anything, even something as delicious and innocuous as one of Clara's smoothies, made me want to yak.

I shook my head again, unable to talk. Clara took me by the hand and led me to my bed. Then she tucked me in and went away for a minute before coming back with a cool washcloth, which she lay on my forehead.

"I don't understand," I said. I'd been lying on my side, but now I rolled onto my back and looked up at her. "I just don't understand what I did wrong."

Clara shook her head. "Don't think like that," she said. "You didn't do anything wrong."

I was too tired to explain myself, but I knew I was on to something. Max loved me, then Max didn't love me. You don't just fall out of love with someone for no reason. I needed to retrace our steps, figure out how we'd gotten from Point A to Point Breakup. How else could we go back to where we'd been?

"You don't understand," I said. But Clara cut me off.

"Shh," she said. She flipped over the washcloth so the cool side was against my forehead. If I hadn't been so tired, I would have told her she'd make a great mom.

"Shh," she said again. She stood up. "I'll be right back."

I wanted to tell her she didn't have to come back, but suddenly I was so exhausted I could barely even form the thought, much less the words.

So I don't know if she ever did end up coming back because the next thing I knew, it was morning.

For the first few seconds right when I woke up, I must have still been half asleep because I didn't remember what had happened the night before. I felt sad and my eyes felt swollen and sore, and I know this is a total cliché but it's *true*—I just thought, *I must have had a bad dream*. Only, then I rolled over and saw the washcloth lying on the floor next to my bed, and everything came rushing back, and I knew I hadn't dreamed a bad dream.

I was living one.

THREE

. . .

You Go, Girlfriend!

"You're not going to quit the newspaper, honey, are you?"

"God, Mom, of course not. Thanks for your vote of confidence."

My mom had managed to feign sympathy about my breakup for exactly 2.5 seconds. By eleven thirty Saturday morning, en route to my nana's for brunch, she'd switched into high gear on her Sisterhood Is Powerful routine.

"I'm really glad you have friends like Martha and Clara," she said. Unfortunately, sometimes moms are their most annoying when saying things you actually agree with. I flipped on the radio, hoping she'd take the hint and be quiet. Luckily a classical station came on; I was pretty sure that for the rest of my life I'd have to listen to songs composed hundreds of years before I was born, the only body of music in existence that didn't remind me of Max.

"Maybe you'd like to come to my next book club meeting with me," she offered, reaching over and patting me on the knee. "Didn't you read *The Sun Also Rises* in English last year?"

"Mom, *please*," I said. The prospect of a night with a bunch of bitter, middle-aged women didn't exactly cheer me up. "I'd rather kill myself."

Hearing I'd rather be dead than spend an evening with her and her friends seemed to diminish my mom's desire not only to cheer me up but to speak to me. As we drove in silence, I stared out the window, thinking of my dad. He was in China with his boyfriend, visiting a factory where they mass-produce bamboo planks, the new material my dad is into working with (he owns a furniture design company). I totally love my dad's boyfriend, who refers to himself as my wicked stepmother, but the happiness my dad and Jay have found together suddenly struck me as insidious. What if in every breakup, the dumper gets to live happily ever after (*Love! Travel!*), while the dumpee gets a lifetime membership in The Bitter Book Club?

♥ ♥ ♥

"Darling, I was starting to get worried." My grandmother was standing at the open door, waving to us. For a grandma, she's pretty young looking. She goes to an exercise class three times a week at the Y, and she has these friends from the neighborhood she walks with every other morning. They call themselves "The Ladies."

"Hi, Mom," called my mom, stepping out of the car.

"Hi, Nana."

She came down the porch steps and practically suffocated me with her bear hug. "Oh, sweetheart, how *are* you?"

"I'm okay, Nana," I lied. I love my nana, but I wasn't exactly in the mood to get a lecture on life and love from my seventy-year-old grandmother. The only boyfriend Nana ever had was my grandpa Harry, who died when I was two. They started going out during, like, the Eisenhower administration, which limits Nana's ability to grasp the more subtle aspects of twenty-first century romance. Exhibit A: When Max and I first got together, Nana asked if we were going to get pinned.

"Jennykins. My little Jennykins." She was still hugging me, only now we were rocking slightly back and forth. It was like the least romantic slow dance in the history of the human race.

Finally, she pulled away and took my face in both her hands. "He's a terrible boy," she said. "He's a terrible boy to do such a thing to you."

"Nana, he didn't *do* anything so bad." It was

hard to talk with her pressing my cheeks together.

"Don't defend him," she said. "I always thought he was a nothing."

I knew Nana was trying to cheer me up, but telling me the person I'd been in love with for five months (and crushed out on for two years before that) is a "nothing" wasn't exactly comforting. It's bad enough being dumped by a smart, funny, popular guy who edits the *Spectator* and got in early to Harvard. Now I'd been rejected by a nothing?

What did that make me—a less-than-nothing?

As we walked inside, my grandmother pointed out a wooden table she'd had stripped and refinished and a new rug she'd bought. My mother said they were both nice. She ran her hand over the table and nodded at its smooth veneer. "They did a good job."

"Tom recommended them," said my grandmother. Then she added defensively, "I asked you for a name, but you never gave me one. So I called Tom."

Tom is my dad, and the furniture design company he currently runs is one he and my mom created together and he bought her out of after the divorce (which is when she went back to teaching graphic design at Parsons)—thus my grandmother's assumption that at least one of them would know someone who could refinish a table.

Maybe because she felt disloyal for having talked to my dad, or maybe because she just gets frustrated with my mom, my grandmother stayed on the offensive. "Tom *must* know some nice single men in Manhattan. They can't *all* be gay. Maybe he could introduce you to someone."

"Mother, *please*. I'm not having my ex-husband play matchmaker." They were both looking at the table instead of each other and shaking their heads, like it was the wood that had disappointed them, not one another.

When they stand next to each other, you can tell that my mom and Nana are mother and daughter. Nana's hair is gray now, but it used to be blond, like my mom's, and they both have bright green eyes; in pictures of Nana when she was my mom's age, it's obvious why Grandpa Harry fell in love with her at first sight and asked her to marry him on their second date.

It's pretty depressing when you find yourself thinking that maybe if you looked more like your grandmother, your boyfriend wouldn't have dumped you.

"Well, I guess that's water under the bridge, anyway," said Nana. She tucked her hand under my arm and steered me out of the foyer and into the dining room, where the table was set for an elaborate lunch. Seeing the individual bowls of fruit salad made me dizzy with nausea. How was I possibly going to get through this meal? This day? This life? I could feel tears burning behind my eyes. In a second I was going to start bawling.

I slipped my arm free. "I—" Before I could finish my sentence with *have to jump off the roof*, my cell rang. "—have to get that," I said instead.

Max. It had to be Max. I practically bodychecked my mother to get to my phone.

But when I flipped open my phone, it wasn't Max's name displayed, it was Martha's. And even though I knew she was calling because Clara had told her about me and Max and she wanted to make sure I was okay, and even though I don't need my mom to tell me how lucky I am to have friends like Martha and Clara because I *know* how lucky I am, I just hit IGNORE and snapped the phone shut. I told myself it was because Nana doesn't like it if people take calls when they're supposed to be visiting, but really it was because I didn't think I could talk through the ocean of sadness that washed over me when I saw MARTHA and not MAX on my screen. I put the phone in the side pocket of my bag and returned to the table.

"Sweetheart, how do you children ever relax with those things ringing in your ear every five minutes?"

"It doesn't ring every five minutes, Nana," I said sharply. And then I felt terrible. It wasn't enough I'd just ignored a call from my best friend, now I was snapping at my nana.

27

Who was this person I'd become, and what had she done with Jennifer?

Nana ignored my tone and gestured to the seat opposite hers. I sat down.

"Now, darling, your mother told me everything," she said, reaching across the table for my hand and gently patting it. "Are you *really* going to be all right?"

Nana's something of a worrier (okay, full disclosure: she believes fresh air + wet hair = death). Since she already loses enough sleep over my well-being, I tried my best to inject some enthusiasm into my answer. "I'm going to be fine, Nana. Really."

She narrowed her eyes in my direction. "A breakup is the single most traumatic event in the life of a woman outside of a death. Some women can take *years to recover*." Was it my imagination or did Nana look over at my mother as she said years to recover? She rapped the table before continuing. "I *do not* want you to lose years to that boy."

It would have been nice if my grandmother refusing to say Max's name was some kind of statement about just how diabolical she found him, but I was pretty sure she'd never been one hundred percent clear on what his name was. When we were together, she sometimes called him Mark or Mike by mistake, then once she called him Tom (which, when you think about it, is so completely gross you really *can't* think about it), and after that she just called him "that nice young man of yours," as in, *So, how is that nice young man of yours?*

"Nana, you sound like some kind of relationship expert," I said.

My grandmother sat up straighter and smiled, as if she had a secret. "Maybe I am," she said and popped a melon ball in her mouth. Then she swallowed, reached behind her, and took a brightly wrapped package off the breakfront. "Here," she said. She held it out to me across the table.

"What is it?" I asked.

"Open it and see," she said, smiling at me.

Nana's pretty cool, but she doesn't exactly have the best fashion sense, and she really loves giving jewelry and clothes as gifts. For my last birthday, she gave me socks with reindeer wearing *actual bells* and a turquoise sweater with black sleeves that, by law, I could only wear on a flying trapeze. Usually I can fake enthusiasm for one of her gifts, but today I wasn't sure I'd be able to pull it off.

I slipped my finger under the tape, careful not to rip the paper so that Nana could reuse it, which she enjoys doing. I was so busy trying to simultaneously preserve the paper and work my face into an expression of fake delight that it took me a minute to register the actual gift. When I finally did, I realized that, incredibly enough, my nana had found the pen-and-paper equivalent of the circus sweater.

The cover was pink. Shocking pink. It was so pink it seemed to throb with pinkness. Smack in the middle was a raised, gold heart, split in two by a pink lightning bolt. Above the heart, in white, capital letters, was the book's title.

The Breakup Bible.

I was too horrified to speak. Luckily, Nana started talking. "I was listening to *Fresh Air* yesterday"—I know Nana's addicted to NPR, but my impression was that they mostly interviewed people who wrote books like *1492: Year of Discovery, Year of Loss*—"and *who* should be on but Doctor . . . Doctor . . ." she paused and wrinkled her forehead.

I read the name she was searching for off the cover. "Emory Emerson."

Nana snapped her fingers as if she'd answered her own question. "Dr. Emory Emerson. And she says there's no reason a woman can't get over a breakup *very* quickly if she'll just follow a few basic rules."

By now I'd opened the book and was looking at the inside flap. "Commandments," I said. My voice sounded flat and distorted to my ears, like I was speaking underwater.

"What's that, darling?"

"The book calls them commandments." I read to her, "'*The Breakup Bible*'s Ten Commandments can make you the happiest dumpee on the block.'" I looked up. Nana was smiling across the table at me.

"Is that a coincidence or is that a coincidence?" she said. "Yesterday I hear Dr. Emerson on the radio, and this morning your mother calls me and tells me about you and . . ." She gestured vaguely. "The *second* I hung up the phone, I went out and bought the book." She paused for a minute, then spoke again. "You go, girlfriend," she said. She spoke as if there were nothing unusual about what she had just said, as if she'd just asked me to pass her the ketchup.

"Nana?" I said.

My grandmother repeated herself. "You go, girl-friend." She was smiling, and her voice was animated, but the inflection was completely wrong, like she had learned English by studying a Berlitz tape. I wasn't sure if I wanted to laugh or to bang my head against the table until men in white coats arrived to cart me away.

Nana's smile faded a little and she looked nervously from me to my mother. "Am I saying it wrong? That's what Dr. Emerson said." She cocked her head and stared at a point over my shoulder. "Or maybe it was, 'You go, *my* friend.'"

My mom, who doesn't exactly spend her free time downloading Jay-Z off iTunes, looked confused. "I don't know which is right, Mom," she said. "Maybe it depends on the situation."

I knew this was funny. I knew that if this conversation had taken place *last* Saturday instead of today, I would have been laughing too hard to dial the phone to call Max to repeat it to him, and as soon as I'd started telling it, he would have started laughing too hard to hear me and I would have needed to keep starting over.

This is heartbreak, I thought. *Knowing something is funny but not being able to laugh.*

And now I knew I was going to start crying for real. I stood up. "Thanks for the book, Nana. I'm going to go read it right now."

My grandmother gave a little clap of happiness. "I just *knew* it was the perfect gift."

My eyes began to water. I turned away from the table so fast I almost knocked over my chair. It teetered for a second before righting itself. "Careful, darling," said Nana. "Don't hurt yourself."

"I'm okay," I said. I kept my back to her, but I couldn't do anything about the quiver in my voice except hope she didn't notice it. "I'll be in the living room."

"Enjoy it, darling," my grandmother called after me.

♥ ♥ ♥

How *The Breakup Bible* could call itself a self-help book was beyond me, since the only thing it was helping me do was see the advantage of suicide. The introduction was titled Honey, It's Over. O-V-E-R, Over!, and in case you failed to get the message, the final chapter was titled Table for One—How You Can Live Happily Ever After Alone! There were a slew of commandments you were supposed to follow, scattered between chapters with titles like He's Moved On and So Should You! and Great Dumpees in History—Who Knew You Had so Much in Common with Catherine of Aragon?!

Long before my mom came into the living room to tell me my brother, Danny, might have broken his arm at his hockey game and was waiting for us in the emergency room at White Plains Hospital, I'd given up on *The Breakup Bible*, slipping it into my bag and removing my cell phone. *Call me*, I whispered to my Nokia, hoping to telepathically reach Max, *Call me*.

But of course, he didn't.

FOUR

. . .

GOOD-BYE, MR. WRONG!

IT TURNED OUT THAT THE ONLY THING more
depressing than lying on Nana's couch was sitting in the
emergency room.

The February day, which had started out crisp and
sunny and unseasonably mild even by global warming
standards, had turned cold and rainy by the time we'd
parked. Inside were more than a dozen people who had
either received or were about to receive bad news. I
know my proximity to pain and death should have made
me feel grateful that all I had going wrong in my family
was a broken heart (mine) and a potentially broken arm
(Danny's), but being surrounded by so much grief only
made me that much sadder. Some misery loves company; mine, apparently, didn't.

We spotted Danny sitting at the end of a row of

empty chairs next to a guy with glasses. Danny was holding his right arm gingerly, but when he saw us, he sat up straighter and gave a nod, like it was nice we'd stopped by but he didn't really need us there.

"Oh, honey, what happened?" My mom sat in the empty chair next to Danny and tried to put her arm around him.

"Mom, chill, okay?" he said, shrugging her off. "It's not that big a deal." He looked up at me through his bangs. "Hey, babe," he said. "How's it going?"

"Okay." I pointed at his arm. "Does it hurt?"

"Nah," he said. Then he gestured at the glasses man. "This guy's just being a total sissy."

The guy rolled his eyes at my mom and me and smiled. "Apparently only sissies seek medical care." He extended his hand to my mom. "I'm Evan Green," he said. "My son's on the team with Danny."

My mother reached across Danny and shook Mr. Green's hand. "Karen Lewis," she said. "Thank you for waiting here with Danny."

The theme from *Shaft* blasted us all into an abrupt silence. Danny reached into his pocket and checked to see who was calling, then stood up. "Gotta take this, folks," he said, stepping away from his chair. "Can't keep the ladies waiting."

Lately my thirteen-year-old brother has started

acting like a cross between Austin Powers and Ludacris. If there's a girl within fifty miles of him, he's gotta be all suave and *Hey, baby, how ya doin'?* If there are no females in the vicinity, he's talking with his "homies" about "chicks" and "hotties" and whether or not girls they know are "fly" or "woof!" It's totally gross, which I tell him more or less hourly, to zero effect. Dad says Danny's probably worried that since his dad is gay, he might be gay, too. He thinks Danny's overcompensating, trying to show he's a man (which is hilarious, considering he's about five feet tall), and that he'll get over it and I should just ignore this phase, which is easier said than done. I mean, how can you ignore it when your little brother greets you each morning with *You're lookin' fresh today, sistah.* For a while he was even saying stuff like *That shirt ain't workin' for you, babe. If you want the customer to make a purchase, you gotta show off the merchandise.* Finally, I told him it was really gay to talk about women's fashion, so at least he's stopped rating my wardrobe.

"Listen, stud," said Mr. Green as Danny put the phone up to his ear. "Just don't stray too far. They're going to take us into X-ray soon."

Danny waved Mr. Green's comment away like it was an ugly girl he couldn't be bothered to talk to and took his phone across the room.

"Well, it was certainly nice of you to wait with

Danny," said my mom. I could tell she was embarrassed by Danny's whole "It's Hard Out There for a Pimp" routine. "I can't thank you enough."

"I'm glad to help," he said, standing. "In fact, I need to make a phone call myself. I'll be back in a second."

My mom stood up, too. "There's really no need. I wouldn't want you to waste any more of your day than you already have."

He smiled at her. "I did my residency under the guy who's head of orthopedics here," he said. "I think I can save you some time if I stick around."

"Well, that's very nice of you, but . . ." she looked pointedly around the crowded room. "I think it will be a long wait."

"Give me a minute," said Mr.—or, I guess, Dr.—Green. "Let me see what I can do."

♥ ♥ ♥

My mother was being pretty civil to Dr. Green, considering she usually gets irate if someone (i.e. Nana) even *implies* that it's okay to ask for help if you need it. Twice she actually thanked him for how he was speeding up the whole emergency room process; but if we were experiencing the express version, I shudder to think what the local is like. The time dragged by. I tried having a conversation with Danny, but all he would talk about was how he hoped some babelicious nurse would give him a sponge bath. I was about to ask my mom if I could take the car and Dr. Green could drive her and Danny home, but then she started asking Dr. Green again to please not waste any more of his day on us, and I knew she wasn't about to let me do something that would mean he had no choice but to stay until Danny was treated.

♥ ♥ ♥

By the time Danny was called down to X-ray, I'd talked to Martha (twice) and Clara (once), comparison shopped the vending machines, counted the ceiling tiles, and listened to my brother say, "Yo, homey, what up?" into his phone roughly fifty times. There was absolutely nothing left for me to do but look at the sad faces of all the broken-down people surrounding me and wonder if I looked like them.

I missed Max. I wanted to call Max. How pathetic was I, wanting to call the guy who'd dumped me? What did I think he was going to say if I called him? "Jennifer, thank God you called! I was temporarily abducted by aliens, and I have the feeling the pod person left to inhabit my body may have broken up with you."

Well, okay, maybe he wouldn't say that. But didn't he miss me? He had to miss me. It's not possible for one person to miss another person so much she thinks she might die, and for that other person not to even miss her at *all*, is it? I mean, we'd been soul mates. Soul mates are forever.

Aren't they?

I called Clara again but got her voice mail. Ditto Martha. When I put my phone back into my bag, the pink cover of *The Breakup Bible* throbbed at me, and I was so bored I actually thought about *reading* it. And who knew? Maybe Dr. Emory Emerson *could* help. According to the book jacket, more than a million people had bought *The Breakup Bible*. Could a million people be wrong?

Aah . . . yeah.

I looked around the room for something else to read. On a faux-wood table next to my chair was an old issue of *Car and Driver*, which had fallen open to an article titled, "Are You Using the Right Brand of Motor Oil?"

I took Dr. Emerson's book out of my bag and cracked it open to page one.

Introduction: Honey, It's Over. O-V-E-R, OVER!
If you've bought this book, congratulations! You've taken the first step toward realizing you're too good for that scumbag you used to call your boyfriend,

lover, best friend, significant other . . . even husband. You know Mr. Wrong is never coming back, and you're ready to MOVE ON WITH YOUR LIFE. Well, all I can say to that is, *You go, girlfriend!* A fabulous, foxy lady such as yourself knows when it's time to say good riddance to bad rubbish!

It had been bad enough when Max was "nothing." Now he was a scumbag? I'd been dumped by "bad rubbish"? So far Dr. Emerson wasn't exactly making me feel like a million bucks.

Okay, first things first. I want you to take out a pen and write down your ex's top five faults—I know you'll probably have trouble stopping at five, but that's all we have room for right now ☺. Go on, use the space on this page, and write in BIG, BOLD letters.

Was I really going to write in a book? A hardcover book? A brand-new hardcover book? I took a pen out of my bag and stared at the page.

Maybe she didn't have as much confidence in her readers as her exclamation points implied because under the numbers, Dr. Emerson had listed some suggestions for those of us suffering from writers' block.

Remember how he left his dirty socks on the floor? And what about that stupid joke he told over and over again? God, aren't you glad you won't have to hear *that* one ever again? At last, no need to race home on Sundays in time for the "big game." And be honest—are you really going to miss listening to his snoring night after night? And how about all those times he cheated on you? Don't you think a lady as fabulous as you deserves a guy who can be faithful?

Did Max leave his socks on the bathroom floor? Did he snore? Dr. Emerson didn't seem to have much advice for people who hadn't been cohabitating. I looked at her other suggestions. Did Max even *tell* jokes? Nobody I knew actually told jokes, except a few of my teachers sometimes. And what "games" was Max supposedly watching? The reason we'd had to race home on Sundays was my curfew.

The only bad thing I could think of that Max had done was break up with me. And it wasn't like I could write "Dumped Me" next to number one. "Dumping Jennifer" wasn't a fault, like leaving your dirty socks lying around or snoring. (Actually, now that I thought about it, I wasn't really sure about snoring, either. Wasn't that, like, a biological condition? If you could put "snoring," did that mean you could put "blindness" or say something like, "I'm just glad I won't have to push that wheelchair around anymore"?)

The slight hope I'd had that Dr. Emerson might be able to ameliorate my situation was fading fast.

And would it have *killed* him to remember your birthday? I mean, come on! Birthdays only come once a year. It's not like he had to remember yours every damned week.

For my birthday, which is in November, Max gave me the best present I've ever gotten—a fake article he'd written and had framed. It was supposedly cut out of *The New York Times*, and it was a profile of me, Jennifer Lewis, the Pulitzer Prize–winning journalist who had just published her best-selling memoirs. According to the article, I was one of the most famous reporters in the world; my name was a household word. Which wasn't surprising considering I'd basically interviewed every major head of state on the planet, covered every significant political event of the previous thirty years, and now, in addition to teaching journalism at Columbia University, I consulted for a hit television series about the life of the First Lady (*The East Wing*). According to the article, I also ran a liberal-leaning think tank in Washington, D.C., while continuing to contribute articles to *The New Yorker*, *Harper's* and, occasionally, *The New York Review of Books*.

The whole thing must have taken forever to make; the production alone (he'd set up the document using the font and layout of *The New York Times Magazine*) would have involved hours of work, not to mention the actual writing. He'd even scanned in a photo. In between the two columns of text was a picture of me from when I was about eight, wearing a bikini with little strawberries on it and a ginormous sun hat of my mom's. The caption read, ACE REPORTER LEWIS IN HER SALAD DAYS.

"Hey," I said when I saw the picture, "where'd you get this?"

"From the collage on your wall." He was smiling; you could tell he was really proud of having pulled the whole thing off. "I put it back, too."

Maybe some girls would be freaked out by the fact that their boyfriend had managed to steal a picture off the wall without their noticing. And maybe those same girls would have wanted jewelry or clothing, or they would have been mad that their boyfriend didn't take them out for a fancy dinner or get them a dozen roses or do some other traditional "I love you" birthday thing.

But I don't wear jewelry, and I don't need clothes, and I think I would just about barf if some guy gave me a bunch of flowers that were going to be dead in a week.

Plus—and I know you're not supposed to think about things like this, but sometimes you can't help it—Max's family is rich. Really rich. Like, he used to joke that he'd gotten into Harvard because his parents donated the money to build a dorm, but even though he was kidding (I think), they definitely *could* have donated the money for something like that. He lives in a huge mansion right on the Sound, and the Mini Cooper he drives is brand-new, and when his family flies somewhere on vacation, they take a *private plane*.

So the point is that if Max had gotten me something really expensive like a designer bag or a cashmere sweater, it would have been nice, I guess, but it would have been like, whatever. He could afford to buy me about ten of each every day. He could afford to buy *every girl at Hillsdale* about ten of each every day.

Which is why his birthday present was so out-of-this-world crazy amazing. It was like he'd chosen to give me the one thing it wasn't easy for him to give me. And it was so funny and so smart and so *Max*. I know De Beers says a diamond is forever, but if you ask me, a fake profile from *The New York Times* is forever. A diamond is for everyone.

The only problem with his present, the only one, tiny thing I didn't like, was the part where the article referred to "a job she took after divorcing her first husband, Max Brown, who left journalism to attend Harvard Business School."

"Wait," I said, reading that part for the second time. "Why do we have to get divorced?"

I was sitting cross-legged on my bed, holding the framed interview in my lap, and he was lying down next to me, his head propped up on his hand.

"Well, clearly you end up outclassing me," he said. "You're the star reporter and I go and work for my daddy like a total lameass."

"Why can't we both be star reporters?" I asked.

He pulled me down next to him. I had to move fast to keep from whacking him in the head with the picture frame, but then we were lying face-to-face. Max kissed my nose. "Why can't we all just get along?" he asked. Then he kissed my throat and my ear before suddenly rolling me over on my back and pinning me.

"Hey," I said, laughing. "No fair."

"Do you like your present?" he asked, grinning. He was holding my wrists and sitting on me.

"Do we have to get divorced?" I asked, grinning back at him.

"Only if you wise up and leave me for your career," he said. He lowered his head and kissed me once, twice. Then he let go of my wrists and I wrapped my arms around him.

"Not a chance," I said, and we spent the rest of the afternoon listening to The Shins and making out on my bed.

♥ ♥ ♥

I blinked, realizing I'd been staring at the page in front of me without seeing it for way too long. Then I looked up and tried to focus my eyes on something else. Across the aisle from me, a couple that looked to be in their early twenties was bickering. I couldn't hear what they were saying, but the man kept pointing at his wrist and the woman kept putting her hands up like, *Well, what do you expect me to do?* Finally they stopped speaking and just stared straight ahead, each clearly wishing the other would disappear.

They weren't horrible looking, but they weren't exactly attractive. He was starting to go bald, and she had dark circles under her eyes and thin, brittle-looking hair. You could tell he snored and left his dirty socks on the floor and made her rush home so he could watch the "big game" every Sunday. And even if he didn't forget her birthday, he probably didn't buy her what she wanted. Like, she was definitely the kind of girl who would have been really happy to get roses and a heart-shaped pendant with little diamond chips on it, but he probably bought her season tickets to the Giants or some kitchen appliance so she could cook him better meals.

Why would a couple like that stay together when Max and I had broken up? We *never* fought. We *never* sat next to each other staring into space and hating one another. We'd never even had a *misunderstanding*.

Out of the corner of my eye, I saw my mom and Danny and Dr. Green come into the main waiting area. Danny had a cast on his arm, and even from this distance, I could see the big red heart one of the "babe-licious" nurses must have drawn for him.

My mom waved to me, and I stood up, leaving Dr. Emerson's book on the table next to *Car and Driver*. Maybe the blond with split ends could use it to get over her lame, balding boyfriend. Probably lots of women who came into this emergency room could use a book that would help them forget their lying, cheating, birthday-forgetting, dirty-sock-on-the-floor-leaving, snoring boyfriends and husbands.

But how do you get over a non-lying, non-cheating, non-birthday-forgetting guy? Dr. Emerson's advice was all fine and good if you wanted to forget Mr. Wrong, but it didn't do much good if you needed to forget Mr. Right.

Unfortunately, I'd gone about halfway to the exit when I heard someone yelling, "Hey! Hey!"

I turned around. Split Ends was waving in my direction, and when she saw she'd gotten my attention, she pointed at the table where *The Breakup Bible* was.

"You forgot your book." She smiled at me in this way that clearly said, *I'm really sorry you got dumped.*

She pitied me. A girl with horrible hair and a boyfriend who needed a *serious* prescription for extra-strength Rogaine *pitied* me. *Me!* I went back and picked up the book, giving her a smile that I hoped said, *I'm sorry about your life.*

Unfortunately, she was giving me the same smile.

FIVE

· · ·

HELLO, HAPPINESS!
(WHY YOU'RE FEELING BETTER ALREADY)

"I CAN'T DO THIS." I turned away from the *Spectator* door and squeezed into the small recess where the water fountain was.

"You *can* do this," hissed Clara. Her eyes seemed to burn through her glasses. "Stop it."

I hung my head. "I can't. I can't." I looked up at her. "Why did he break up with me?"

"Because he's *retarded*," she said.

I was going to cry again. "He's not retarded," I said. "He's smart. He's going to Harvard."

"His daddy went to Harvard," she said. "And then he donated a lot of money so his faux-radical son with the affected interest in music could go there, too. It's so lame it makes me want to puke." Clara wants to be a litigator when she grows up, and all I can say is, good luck to the opposing team.

I dug my fingers into my scalp and pulled on my hair, hoping the physical pain would make the emotional pain less intense. "Remember when he MapQuested the route from my house to Harvard Yard? Why would you do something like that and then break up with someone? What did I do?" I was going to start sobbing right there in the four-hundreds corridor.

"You didn't *do* anything," said Clara. "Listen to me. He's a total loser. He's going to go to Harvard—just like his daddy—and then he's going to go to Harvard Business School—just like his daddy—and then he's going to become one of those corrupt CEOs who live in Greenwich, Connecticut, and buy themselves a red convertible when they turn fifty, and the whole time he'll think of himself as this radical dude because he once listened to a bootlegged Hysterics concert back in high school."

I was impressed by how angry Clara sounded. Was she *really* mad, or was she just acting mad to make me feel better? Either way, it was almost working.

"You are fabulous," she continued, kneading my shoulders like she was my coach and I was a heavyweight fighter about to go back into the ring. "You just have to make it through the next two hours. I'm going home to walk the dog, Martha's meeting you here at five, and then you're both coming to my house for dinner."

"Okay," I said. How pathetic was I? What was next, Clara and Martha tucking me in with warm milk and a story?

She put her arms around me and gave me a hug. "You are *so* much better than that loser," she said. "And you look *awesome*, if I do say so myself." She and Martha had coordinated my look via cell phone Sunday night. According to them, jeans, a black turtleneck sweater, and my motorcycle boots shouted, "I am woman, hear me roar!"

"Thanks." It came out very *I am woman, hear me mumble,* but Clara didn't say so; she just smiled and waved as she started down the hall. I took a deep breath, ran my fingers through my hair, and pushed open the door.

Max was sitting at a computer on the other side of the room; just the sight of his back almost made me sink to my knees. He was wearing a red sweater we'd picked out together at Banana Republic. Did he remember that I'd helped him choose it? Was that why he'd worn it today, to tell me he was sorry, that he'd made a terrible mistake, that he wanted me back? Or did he not remember the day he bought it, how in the store he'd pulled me against his chest and asked if it was soft enough?

The thought that he might not even remember was like a punch in the stomach.

"Hi, Jen." I turned to my right, where Anya Cates was standing. Anya's a writer Max promoted to contributing editor in January, after Doug Sandler, who got into Brown early, said he didn't "want to do the *Spectator* anymore." Max, who heard from Harvard right before Doug heard from Brown, was *furious*. He went on and on about people who just write for the paper because they want to impress colleges, then drop it as soon as they're accepted. The funny thing is, when Anya, who's a junior, offered to take over for Doug, I couldn't help thinking the only reason *she* wanted the position was because it would look good on her college applications. I mean, she's traditionally been one of our most unreliable writers; I doubt she even knows what the word deadline means. Max and I used to make fun of how, whenever Doug or I or one of the other editors would point out that an article of hers was overdue, she'd stand there, staring at us and sucking on a piece of hair (she has this totally wild black hair that falls about halfway down her back that she pretends to find annoying—as in, "God, I *totally* need a haircut, my hair's *soo* annoying"—but that she clearly thinks is the sexiest thing since the string bikini). Then she'd go, "Wait, what's today?" like, *I'm just* waay *too cute and flaky to be expected to master the days of the week.*

So it wasn't like she was exactly a natural for the

position. I kind of got the feeling Max gave it to her as a way to say, *Screw you, Doug*, since Doug had always complained about having to chase Anya down to get articles from her. Lately, of course, *I* was the one who was screwed, since the privilege of chasing Anya down when her articles were due had fallen largely to me. Even before we broke up, I was annoyed at Max for not seeing how his *Screw you* to Doug rebounded onto yours truly.

"Hi, Anya," I said.

At the sound of my voice, Max spun around in his chair and looked over at me. I looked back at him, amazed that I was still standing.

"Hey," he said, so quietly I wouldn't have heard it if I hadn't been staring right at him.

"Hey," I said.

Did everyone else know? Mr. Barton said something about getting the meeting started, and as we all grabbed chairs and pulled up to the big table in the middle of the room, I found myself trying to figure out who knew about me and Max, and who didn't, by looking around the table for an I'm-so-sorry-for-you stare. Anya, naturally, had too much hair in her face to give me any kind of stare at all. Todd had his head down, reading something. Malcolm, Gordon, Leslie, and Sarah, the contributing editors, didn't seem to be looking at me strangely. I decided our breakup was still under wraps.

"So," said Mr. Barton, folding his arms across his chest and leaning back in his chair, "what's news?"

I tuned out as everyone talked about the progress of the March issue. Editorial meetings have been way more heated this year than last year, since Mr. Barton's really committed to giving the board the freedom to decide for ourselves which issues to cover in the *Spectator*. Unfortunately (or fortunately, depending on your feelings about mortal combat), there's some conflict about how to utilize that freedom. As editor in chief, Max wants the paper to focus less on Hillsdale and more on national and international issues, which Gordon and Sarah are also into. Todd and Leslie, on the other hand, think it's important to cover more school-related things. The problem is, Todd and Leslie don't necessarily agree on what "school-related" means. For example, back in October, Todd wanted to do an in-depth profile of everyone who was running for the school board. Leslie, meanwhile, has been campaigning for a gossip column.

The truth is, even though I think Leslie's ridiculous, I probably fall more into her and Todd's camp than Max's. I'm not that interested in stuff like eco-summits in Malaysia—the one time I did a piece on a coup in Latin America, it felt more like writing a research paper than reporting a news story. At the same time, I think it's cool how interested in the world Max is, and how he thinks it's important for us to educate the Hillsdale population about international events.

Normally I get really into the arguments we have at editorial meetings. I've always wanted to be a journalist, ever since I was ten and my dad and I watched *All the President's Men*, a movie about these two reporters, Carl Bernstein and Bob Woodward, who uncovered Watergate, which is a scandal named for the Watergate complex in Washington, D.C., where the Republicans broke into the Democratic National Committee headquarters not long before the 1972 presidential election. Because of Woodward and Bernstein's investigation, it was discovered that President Nixon had been involved in the break-in, and he had to resign. I love that two low-level reporters, by working hard and not taking no for an answer, could bring down a corrupt president of the United States.

Today, though, I stayed out of the discussion. I kept remembering how at last week's meeting, Max and I had sat next to each other and played footsie under the table, which, even though we knew it was totally unprofessional and wrong and irresponsible, is what we'd done at almost every editorial meeting since we'd started going out. Once when we were walking to his car after a meeting, Max asked me if Malcolm had said he was going to cover the boy's soccer game that weekend.

"I wasn't keeping track," I admitted. "I thought you were."

"How could I keep track when you had your hand on my knee?" he asked. And then we stopped walking and started making out, and then I pulled away and said, "But who's going to cover the game?" and he started kissing me again and said, "We'll just get it off the wire services," which was so completely hilarious we both started cracking up since "the wire services" like the Associated Press and Reuters and Knight Ridder are huge news agencies that cover major world events, not high school soccer games.

♥ ♥ ♥

I tuned back into the discussion just as Anya said, "Wait, which issue are we talking about again?"

"Next month's," said Malcolm.

"So . . . March, right?"

Max laughed and so did I. He looked over at me. I used my eyes to send him a message. *How can you not still love me when we both think it's funny that Anya doesn't know it's February?*

But then he was making a mark on the page in front of him and looking around the table again. "Thinking ahead, anyone interested in writing on the upcoming elections in Algeria?"

He didn't glance my way again; you'd have thought I was sitting in a different room instead of across the table from him.

"Okay," said Max finally, "I guess I'll cover it. But can you guys try to get *something* to me or Todd or Jen before Friday so it's not the usual last-minute editing crunch?" It wasn't his managing to say my name without looking at me that made me almost start crying right there in front of everybody, it was his calling me Jen. The whole time we were together, he'd never called me Jen. I was always Jenny or Jennifer or JL or J-Lo or Ace Reporter Lewis. Jen was what everybody *else* called me.

Was he everybody else now?

The meeting over, Anya and Malcolm left. Sarah and Mr. Barton stood together reading a draft of her *Othello* review. Max was talking to Gordon, and I heard him say, "Littleton," which is a school we play in basketball. Except for the five of us, there was no one in the room, and except for me, everyone was talking to someone. Not that I could have carried on a conversation to save my life. I bent down and felt around on the floor for my bag.

When I sat up, Max wasn't talking to Gordon anymore. His elbows were on the conference table and he was looking directly at me.

"Hey," he said.

"Hey," I said.

Hadn't we already had this conversation?

"How was your weekend?" he asked.

I didn't need Dr. Emerson to tell me that *I spent it trying not to commit suicide* was the wrong answer. "It was okay," I said. There was a pause. Even back when we were total strangers we hadn't had a conversation this awkward. "Um, how was yours?" I asked.

"It sucked," he said. Then he shook his head sadly.

I almost gasped. His weekend had sucked? *Sucked?* I didn't say anything, just sat there, staring, as he put his legal pad into his backpack and stood up. Was he going to elaborate on this? I stood up, too.

"Reporter Lewis," called Mr. Barton. "Allow me to take a moment of your time, would you?"

No. *NOOOOO!* For a long second, I didn't answer Mr. Barton. Max and I stood and stared at each other.

"Well, I should go," he said finally. He hitched his bag up on his shoulder and made his way around the conference table. When he got to where I was standing, he gave me the gentlest hip check in the history of the world. "Talk to you later."

"Yeah, talk to you later," I repeated, too bewildered to come up with a snappier reply.

Mr. Barton appeared at my side holding a large white envelope. I looked down, but my eyes couldn't process the writing on it. It wasn't until he'd placed the envelope in my hand that I retrospectively registered the familiar font and the words *New York Times* in the return address.

"What does the word internship mean to you?" asked Mr. Barton, dropping into his desk chair.

I looked at him vaguely, like I really *didn't* know what the word internship meant. "What does it *mean?*"

He must have thought I was being ironic because he gave me an appreciative smile before leaning back and putting his feet up on his desk. "Have you ever considered doing one?"

What did Max mean by that hip check? It hadn't even been a *hip check* exactly, more of a gentle leaning into me with a slight bump at the end. Like, *I want to touch you but this is the only way I can get away with it.*

"An internship?" I said finally.

Mr. Barton pulled at his beard in a way that indicated a growing impatience with my irony.

"*The New York Times* has started a summer internship program for high school juniors. Schools can nominate one student who needs to have exhibited"— he started ticking points off on his fingers—"true commitment to journalism, leadership ability, integrity, and a grade point average above B plus. I can testify to everything but the grade point average. Am I wrong in assuming yours meets the requirement?"

I pushed my hair behind my ears and tried to look like someone who was focused on her journalism career. "Um, sorry, what's the requirement again?"

Was Mr. Barton beginning to doubt the wisdom of approaching me with this offer? If so, who could blame him? He dropped his feet to the floor and put his hands on his knees, staring at me. "What's your grade point average, Lewis?"

"I think it's about an A minus." Had he hip-checked me because he thought *I* wanted to touch *him*? Was it his way of touching me without *touching* me? But then why had he said his weekend sucked? Why did he want me to know he'd had a sucky weekend?

"And how would you feel about spending your summer working for the Fourth Estate?"

Summer? How could I know how I wanted to spend my summer when I barely knew how I was going to make it through tomorrow? I was about to say I wasn't sure, when I looked down at my hand and saw the return address on the envelope. *The New York Times. The New York Times.* I took a deep breath. *Focus, Lewis. Focus.*

"Are you asking me if I want to work at the *New York Times* this summer?" I knew that in another place and time this conversation would have made me really, really happy. So happy, in fact, I would have had to stop myself from jumping up and down and screaming like a complete idiot. As it was, my words came out sounding a notch above bored.

Luckily, Mr. Barton's got such a dry sense of humor, he clearly figured this was my way of being understated. "Assuming you're not using the word 'work' in the traditional sense, i.e. labor for which you are financially compensated, the answer is yes."

"Yes," I said. "The answer is yes."

"Great," he said, relaxing back into his chair again. "I'd hoped that's what you'd say." He pointed at the envelope I was holding. "It's a pretty simple application, really. They want a transcript, some articles representative of your work, a letter of recommendation—thank you Mr. Barton—and a 'Why I want to be in journalism' essay of three hundred and fifty words. . . . The usual suspects."

I wasn't processing a word he said. My hip still tingled from the spot where Max had touched it. *Talk to you later.* Was that like, *I'll definitely talk to you later because I'm going to call you later because this weekend I realized how much my life without you sucks and how much I still love you?* Or was it like . . . but I couldn't think what else it could be like.

"The bad news," said Mr. Barton standing up, "is that you have less than two weeks to get your essay written. The application has to be postmarked by February fourteen. That said, I don't think you should use a 'love' stamp."

Valentine's Day. I absolutely could *not* think about Valentine's Day right now.

"If you want any help, let me know," he added, grabbing a stack of papers off the conference table. "Or Max can help you. That's probably the kind of thing you pre-professional kids today find romantic."

Well, that answered my question. Mr. Barton clearly did *not* know Max and I had broken up. Unless we hadn't broken up. Or, well, we'd clearly broken up, but maybe we were about to get back together. So maybe by next week's editorial meeting there wouldn't be anything *to* know.

Thinking about all the knowing and not knowing was making my brain hurt, so it was a huge relief that the door opened and Martha stuck her head in.

"Hey," she said. "Ready to hit the road?" In spite of how confused I was about my conversation with Max, I was still able to feel bummed on Martha's behalf that Todd had left before she got there. Maybe if he'd stayed behind after the meeting, I could have subtly manufactured a way to get them talking, since she hadn't spoken a word to him at the cast party Friday night. That's the problem with Martha and guys—she's so quiet they don't notice she's a total babe. Clearly she and Todd needed a little help if their relationship was ever going to get off the ground, help that yours truly was only too happy to provide.

(Though perhaps the fact that I'd recently been dumped was a sign I should not hire myself out as a professional cupid.)

"Hey, you," I said to her. "I'm coming." I put the application in the front pocket of my bag where it wouldn't get smushed. I'd already turned to leave the room when something Mr. Barton had said finally sank in.

"Yo, Barton?"

"Yes, Lewis?" He was sitting at the computer where Max had been working before the meeting started, but for a miraculous minute I could focus on something other than where Max's posterior had been earlier.

"Did you say the school has to *nominate* someone for this internship?"

He didn't turn around. "I believe I did."

"So you're *nominating* me to work for the *Times* this summer?"

He still didn't turn around. "That is correct."

"Wow," I said, and I actually smiled. "That's really cool."

"Let's try to avoid the word 'cool' in our application, Lewis," he said.

"Will do, Chief."

Martha held the door open for me with her back,

and she gave me a little hug as I walked past her and into the hallway. She had her hair loose around her face, and she was wearing a brightly colored Indian-print skirt and silver, dangly earrings. It really sucked that Todd had left before he could see how pretty she looked.

"Did Mr. Barton nominate you for something?" she asked.

I told her quickly because I didn't want to talk about Mr. Barton, I wanted to talk about Max. Specifically, I wanted to know what she thought about his A) saying his weekend had sucked and B) hip-checking me.

After I'd demonstrated the hip check for the third time so she could see *exactly* what I meant by "soft but not *too* soft," she said, "It definitely means something."

"I think so, too," I said. "But what?"

Martha shook her head. "I don't know." I was really glad I was having this conversation with Martha and not with Clara, whose response to my, *But what?* would undoubtedly have been, *Who cares?* "Maybe he'll call you later and explain," she said.

"Do you think he wants to get back together?" I said.

"If he doesn't, he's *crazy*," said Martha, opening the door to the student parking lot. And even though it was a really nice thing to say, I wished she hadn't said it.

A simple yes would have sufficed.

SIX

• • •

You're Not *Lonely*—You're *Free*!

W HEN THE PHONE HADN'T RUNG by nine, I started
to get a sinking feeling in my stomach. I sat in the den
and channel surfed until I stumbled upon *All the
President's Men*, which would normally have made me
completely psyched but now just made me think of
Max. Not that I hadn't already been thinking about him
(what with the fact that I was always already thinking
about him), but now I had something concrete to
think about *about* him. We must have NetFlixed *All the
President's Men* a dozen times, but somehow we had
never gotten around to actually watching it. In fact,
the last time we'd gotten it and not watched it had
been less than two weeks ago, our last weekend
together (though I didn't know it was our last weekend together at the time, which is kind of ironic,

considering one of the major themes of the movie is the question, *What did the president know and when did he know it?* Turns out Richard Nixon knew a lot more than Jennifer Lewis).

Max's parents were out of town that weekend, and Friday night he went out with his friends. He called me when he woke up Saturday morning, and I went over there and we spent the whole day fooling around and listening to music and basically just being totally in love.

Then we decided it would be fun to have people over. Not a huge party, like most people at Hillsdale have the second their parents go out of town (i.e., Jeremy Peterson); just a few friends, like Jeremy and Michael and Martha and Clara. Almost everyone we called ended up coming, including Anya (who's such a bad driver she almost took out one of Mrs. Brown's rose bushes) and even Doug, whom Max had kind of forgiven for bailing on the paper. In the end, probably about fifteen people were there. The night was perfect. Max's parents have this *huge* wine cellar, and so everyone was sipping wine out of fancy goblets instead of pounding vodka shots like we normally do at parties. It felt like Max and I were a grown-up couple having friends over, not a couple of high school kids taking advantage of having a house to themselves for the weekend.

At some point Max and I went downstairs to get

more wine. We were both pretty drunk, and we started making out, and Max was like, *You should stay over*. Only, I knew if I called my mom and told her I'd had this sudden urge to stay over at Martha or Clara's, she'd totally know something was up. We were kissing up against the rough stone wall of the wine cellar, and through the ceiling you could just hear people laughing and the music playing, and it was like they were upstairs having a party and Max and I were downstairs, all alone in our little cocoon having our *own* party, and I wanted to stay over *so badly*.

So we were kissing, and Max was going, *Stay*, and I was going, *I can't*, and he was going, *Yes you can. If you love me, you'll stay*. And I was laughing and going, *I love you, but I can't stay*, and we were kissing and kissing, and then all of a sudden the basement door opened and Jeremy yelled down, *Did you two die or something?* and we practically flew up the stairs, each of us carrying two bottles of wine. And next thing I knew, it was almost one and I really had to go home. By then we were all sitting in the Browns' great room playing *I Never*, and so Max just gave me a kiss on the cheek and said, *I'll call you tomorrow*.

That's what I don't *get*. I mean, was he planning on breaking up with me *then*? Was he making out with me in his parents' wine cellar, and begging me to spend the night with him and going, *If you loved me, you'd stay*, the whole time thinking, *You know, this relationship just isn't working out*. Because on Friday in the car, he said, "I've been thinking about this *a lot lately*." And "lately" implies at least a week, right? I mean, if you ask me, it implies *way more* than a week, but to be on the safe side, let's just say it implies at *least* a week. And the party was only *six days* before we broke up. Five, if you think about how it was really Sunday by the time I left. I just don't see how it's mathematically possible to be passionately in love with someone on Sunday morning and then just want to be friends with that person on Friday afternoon.

In lieu of answers to my questions, the heavens sent Danny.

"Yo, yo, yo," he said, flopping down next to me and grabbing the remote. "Wassup?" The bright red heart Nurse Babelicious had drawn had faded into a sea of hearts, flowers, hockey sticks, and Get Well Soons the girls of Hillsdale Junior High had no doubt clawed past one another to brand my brother's cast with. I didn't want to begrudge Danny his success with the opposite sex, but right about now I couldn't help being a little depressed by it.

I tapped the sling. "How's your arm?"

He admired his admirers for a minute before returning to channel surfing. "It's all good," he said.

Then, without taking his eyes off the television set, he continued. "So, you and your man. No doubt that's a bummer."

Sometimes talking to Danny makes me feel like Nana. I just want to grab him and yell, *Would you please speak* English! "Um, yeah," I said. "It's a bummer, all right."

"You babes have it rough," he said, shaking his head. Then, gesturing with the remote like it was a microphone, he rapped, "Why do guys hang? Cuz we're after one thang."

"Oh, yeah? And what *thang* is that?"

Danny turned to me, his forehead wrinkled in amazement. "Does the word S-E-X mean anything to you?" He turned back to the television to watch an ad (for what product, I couldn't tell), in which a scantily clad girl emerged from a cloud.

I punched his shoulder. "Does the phrase 'Get a Life' mean anything to *you?*"

Danny's eyes were glued to the screen. It was like he thought next thing the girl was going to emerge from our television. Without looking at me, he responded, "Hey, don't be all up in my face just because Mr. Mini got himself some new booty. I *said* I was sorry."

"Mr. Mini did *not* get himself some new booty," I snapped, grabbing the remote. "And would you mind not *talking* like that?"

Danny shrugged and stood up. "Chill," he said, leaving. "Don't get all PMS on me, woman."

Okay, can I just ask why it is that my brother, whose *every* friend is white, who has absolutely *no* black *acquaintances* even, why is it that this same brother of mine talks like he's recently signed a contract with Roc-A-Fella Records?

Thinking about how white Danny's circle of friends is got me thinking about how I don't really have any black friends either, unless you count Todd, who's not really a friend, just someone I know from the paper. And anyway, Todd doesn't dress or talk like one of the rappers Danny imitates—he never wears baggy jeans or fancy basketball shoes. I wondered if that was just a general sartorial preference or if it had to do with the fact that he doesn't seem to hang out with other black kids at school very much. In fact, now that I thought about it, I realized I *never* saw Todd with another black student. In addition to being on the (all-white) paper, Todd lives in a really fancy neighborhood not far from Max, whereas most of the black students at Hillsdale live in this one area of town that has mostly apartment buildings, not houses.

Thinking about Todd got me thinking about Martha liking Todd. And that got me thinking about how none of us ever said anything about the fact that the guy Martha has a crush on is black. I mean, obviously we *know* he's black. But we know he's a senior, too, and we talk about that. So why didn't we ever talk about Todd's being black?

Maybe that would make a good article for the *Spectator*. Not Martha liking Todd (can you imagine?!), but how race is something we don't talk about at Hillsdale. And it's not like we don't talk about *other* sensitive topics. Like, we talk about sex *all the time*. Even in classes. In English this fall, when we read *Twelfth Night*, we had about a million conversations about gender and cross-dressing and what it means that the "guy" the countess falls in love with is really a girl. For five weeks it was basically sex, sex, sex, sex, sex. And it wasn't just sex in the abstract, either. We had to write a story in which we meet someone at a costume party, start crushing on that person, and then find out the person is really a girl dressed as a guy (or a guy dressed as a girl). So, you know, the whole thing got pretty personal.

But last year when we read *Othello*, we never *once* talked about racism or racial politics, and we definitely didn't write any stories in which we start dating someone we meet at a party who's of a different race. I suddenly realized I didn't even know if Todd was weirded out when he was cast as Othello. I mean, he's never had a lead in a play before. Was Mr. Melnick, the director, just like, *Hey, let's cast the tall black guy as Othello?* If we'd done *The Merchant of Venice,* would he have made sure a Jewish kid played Shylock?

Just as I realized I had the perfect excuse for calling Max, my phone buzzed.

Max!

I threw myself the length of the couch, grabbing my cell. There was a text message.

"how r u? etd china 36 hrs. tonsa bamboo. dinner nyc friday?"

Even though I love my dad, my heart sank. Would I ever again be happy to get a phone call from anyone other than Max?

I avoided answering his "how r u" since my response (suicidal) might have made him worry.

"sure," is what I sent back instead.

Sitting there, holding my cell in my hand, I thought about calling Max. I mean, I did have the perfect excuse. I could just say, *Hey, how's it going? I have this great idea for an article.* And he'd go, *Tell me about it,* and then we'd start talking, and maybe one thing would lead to another, and before you know it he'd . . .

He'd *what?* Beg me to get back together? Tell me breaking up with me was the worst mistake of his life? Just thinking about Max saying, *Well, that sounds like a great idea; we should talk about it at the meeting next week.*

Bye! made me so sad I wanted to die. I flipped the phone shut, then flipped it open and turned it off, just to be sure I, unlike Othello, wouldn't find myself driving a dagger into my own heart.

♥ ♥ ♥

In order to try not to think about Max, I spent the rest of the night thinking about the article, and by morning, I was too excited about the idea to wait until next week's meeting for feedback. At lunch, my first free period of the day, I headed to the *Spectator* office to find Mr. Barton.

The room was pretty quiet for a lunch period. Todd was working on a computer, and Mr. Barton and Leslie were sitting at the conference table editing her "article" ("article") "What's Hot, What's Not: How Are You Spending *Your* Weekend, Hillsdale High?" I dropped into a chair across from them, figuring I was doing Mr. Barton a favor by interrupting.

"Hey," I said.

"Ace Reporter Lewis," said Mr. Barton. Was it my imagination or did he look super relieved to see me?

"Hey, Jen," said Leslie. She smiled at me and ran an acrylic nail–clad hand through her frosted hair. You kind of had to respect how little Leslie cared about the whole "natural beauty" thing.

"Hey," I said. "I'm sorry to interrupt, but I have an idea for an article, and I wanted to run it by you."

"Oh, cool," said Leslie. She gave a little bounce in her seat. "I feel like such an editor now."

I bit my lip briefly to prevent the words *Not you* escaping my mouth. "Well, I was thinking it would be cool to do an exposé . . ." I caught another glimpse of Leslie's headline and decided to turn down the hype. "Actually, exposé's not really the right word. I was thinking more of a study. A discussion, really, about race relations at Hillsdale."

I hadn't realized he could hear me, but suddenly Todd said from across the room, "White man got his boot on the black man's neck." I looked up as he spun around on his chair, and we both started laughing. Then he came over to the table, pulled out a chair, and sat down, and the three of them looked at me.

I felt a little self-conscious, and it wasn't just because there were three pairs of eyes staring at me. It was because one of those sets of eyes was Todd's. But then I reminded myself that my being uncomfortable talking about race in front of a black student was *exactly* the reason I wanted to write the article.

I took a deep breath and continued. "I was thinking about how so many white kids go around dressed like they live in the projects and calling each other, like, 'my homey' and listening to rap and everything. And I thought it might be interesting to talk to some of them about why they do that, and to talk to some of the African American students about whether it bothers them or, you know, what they think about it."

Todd was nodding thoughtfully. "Could open up a whole lot of issues," he said.

"It sure could," said Mr. Barton, who was nodding, too.

"We could do pictures," Leslie piped up. "Like, who looks 'Gangsta Cool' and who looks 'Gangsta Lame.'" She made quotation marks with her fingers when she named each category.

"That wasn't exactly the direction I was thinking of taking this in," I said. I thought my answer was pretty diplomatic considering Leslie's suggestion sounded completely retarded to me. But I knew Mr. Barton was considering making me editor in chief next year, and his hearing me call a fellow editor's idea "completely retarded" probably wasn't an example of the leadership skills that had impressed him enough to nominate me for the *New York Times* internship.

"I'm in," said Todd. Then he added quickly, "I mean, if you want someone to work on it with you."

"That would actually be great," I said. I felt a little less pressure for about a second, which was how long it took me to wonder if it was racist to feel better about writing the article because I'd be writing it with a black student. I made a mental note to consider including that question in the article.

Mr. Barton was tapping his pen against his chin. "I like it," he said. "I think it's important." It was rare for Mr. Barton to say something was important, but when he did, it meant he really thought it was.

♥ ♥ ♥

Okay, full disclosure: it *had* occurred to me that my working on a big, controversial story could be a way to get closer to Max (*Let me run this idea by you, editor to editor. What, you want us to have this discussion in person? Well, if you think that's best. . .*) What *hadn't* occurred to me was the possibility that my working on a big, controversial story could be a way for Martha to get closer to Todd.

But apparently that's just what it was.

On Wednesday Martha and Clara and I were having lunch in the cafeteria when Martha suddenly stopped talking right in the middle of a sentence. Her silence was so abrupt that for a second I actually thought she was choking or something. But then I looked over to where she was looking and saw Todd. He saw us and waved, then said something to one of the guys he was with and started walking toward our table.

"Hey," he said. "Mind if I join you for a minute?"

"Not at all," I said.

It's weird how someone can have this dramatic effect on one person and none whatsoever on someone else. Like, I was perfectly happy to see Todd, but I didn't *care* that he'd sat down with us. Meanwhile, Martha had gone so white it was like there wasn't a drop of blood left in her body. I knew how she felt—if Max had just walked over to our table, it would have been me, not her, in need of CPR—but I couldn't *feel* how she felt. Which is kind of funny when you think about it (though probably not, at that particular moment, to Martha).

"Hi," Todd said to Clara and Martha. Then he added, just to Martha, "Long time no see."

Now instead of looking like death, Martha looked like a Roma tomato. Against her black hair and white T-shirt, the effect of her deep blush was startling.

"Yeah," she said, fiddling with her straw. "Long time no see."

"How've you been?" Todd asked.

Look up. LOOK UP! I concentrated all my psychic energy on Martha, hoping she'd flash him a lingering glance with her baby blues. But all that happened was she looked up at *me.* And her look said, *Please help!*

"What's up?" I asked Todd. He took a long moment

to answer me, which I thought was a good sign. Clearly he was waiting for Martha to answer *him*. Unfortunately, she was too busy studying the nutritional information on the side of her milk carton to see that.

"What's up is, I've taken the liberty of coming up with some preliminary interview questions for this article of yours."

"Article of *ours*," I corrected him.

"Article of *ours*." He inclined his head and smiled. "And I wanted to run them by you. You going to be around the office Friday after school?"

"Yeah, I've got a ton of editing to do. Let's talk then," I said, and Todd stood up. Martha was blushing furiously again, which might have had something to do with how good Todd looked in his jeans.

"Friday," he said.

"Friday," I said.

He lingered by the table, looking at Martha. Unfortunately, only Clara and I saw the small, private smile he was giving her. Finally I kicked her under the table, hard, and she raised her eyes to look at Todd. Catching his expression, she gave him a little smile back. They kept smiling at each other for a long beat, only then someone yelled, "Kincaid, let's get this show on the *road*," and Todd said, "See you guys" and left.

As soon as Todd was out of earshot, I grabbed

Martha's shoulder. "Martha, he is *so* into you," I said. "Did you *see* him?" I stared into Martha's eyes, trying to make my voice as deep as Todd's, which .vas more or less impossible. "'Long time no see.'"

Martha fiddled with her straw, shaking her head. "You don't think he was just being polite?"

"Oh my God," said Clara. "I swear, a guy could, like, drop down on one knee and propose marriage and you'd be all, 'Do you think it means anything?'"

"You're hilarious," said Martha. Then she pushed her sandwich away and looked at me. "So what's the article about anyway?"

I told them about the idea, but my mouth was more or less on autopilot. Because the whole time I was talking, I couldn't stop thinking that if someone could just get Martha and Todd alone in a room together for five minutes, he would *definitely* ask her out. And if that someone was me, maybe, just *maybe*, the insta-karma of the universe would reward my helping Todd and Martha get together by helping me and Max get *back* together.

SEVEN

* * *

ASK YOURSELF, *WHAT DO I WANT IN A MAN?*

With about twenty articles to edit, I hit the *Spectator* office at two forty-five on Friday, planning to stay until it was time to go to the city to meet my dad and Jay for dinner. I'd convinced Martha to stop by on her way home so she could "run into" Todd, but when she got there, he hadn't shown up yet. Then she had to leave, and of course Todd arrived, like, five seconds later. It turned out he and I both had way too much other editing work to do to talk about the article, so we had to schedule another meeting; I tried to secretly factor Martha's schedule in when suggesting good times to meet, but given the way the day had gone thus far, it shouldn't have surprised me that the only time Todd and I were both free was fifth period Monday (when Martha's in class).

The afternoon ended up being a total bust on the romantic front for me, too. Considering the editing crunch we were in, I'd just assumed Max would be at the office working. More than assumed—as the hours passed, I realized that all week I'd been *counting* on seeing him. But even though most of the other editors came by at one point or another, despite the fact that I stuck around until nearly six thirty, long after everyone else had left, he never showed. Finally, I gave up, turned off the computers, and shut the lights, feeling sadder and more defeated than I had since he'd broken up with me, exactly seven days earlier. The fact that he'd made no effort to see or speak to me since Monday's hip check made it hard to convince myself that Max was desperate for a reconciliation.

And then, just as I was trying to figure out how I'd make it through the weekend without knowing if there was any hope at all for our getting back together, right when I was about to start ranking possible excuses for calling him before Monday's *Spectator* meeting, I turned down the corridor that leads to the exit to the student parking lot.

And there was Max.

Is there a Web site called dreamscometrue.com? If so, this moment deserved to be the home page. I almost couldn't believe he was actually standing there; he could easily have been a hallucination willed into existence by the sheer force of my desire to see him.

He was standing with Michael and Jeremy. As much as I wanted to talk to him, I also wanted to show him how cool I was, how if he took me back I wasn't going to be the kind of girlfriend who interrupted him and his friends when they were talking. But I didn't get a chance to demonstrate my Herculean restraint. The second he saw me he said, "Later, guys," and stepped away from them as quickly as if he'd been waiting for me to show up.

"Hey," he said, falling into step alongside me and giving me a gentle push in the shoulder. "Where have you been hiding all week?"

"Oh, I've been around," I said. I could see why people say absence makes the heart grow fonder—Max had never looked as good to me as he did at that minute.

"You leaving?" he asked.

Convinced anything I said would be exactly the wrong thing, I just nodded.

"So," he said, after we'd walked half the length of the corridor in silence.

"So," I said.

He hit the door open with his hip and I followed him outside. It was cold, and he stopped to zip his jacket shut.

I pretty much never bother to zip my jacket; it

always seems like it's easier to be a little cold for a few seconds than to bother taking the time to zip or snap or button your coat up when in less than a minute, you'll just get hot in the car and have to undo whatever you've done. It used to drive Max crazy that I didn't close my coat when we went outside, so what usually happened was he'd zip up his jacket first, then he'd reach over and zip mine.

I put my hands in my pockets while Max finished tucking his scarf into his jacket. Instead of saying anything, he looked at me and shook his head with a rueful smile. Then he reached over and grabbed the bottom of my jacket, carefully fitting the halves of the zipper together.

"How can you not zip your jacket?" he said—it was what he'd always said—smoothly sliding the zipper up to my neck. Then he said, "Look up." I did, and he zipped the neck part closed.

My heart did a long and lovely swan dive down to my ankles. How many weekends had started just like this one, Max zipping my jacket for me as we stood at the edge of the parking lot, talking about our plans for Friday night?

"So," he said again.

"So," *I* said again. Smiling at him, I thought briefly of Dr. Emerson. Clearly she should have called her conclusion, Table for Two: What It Will Feel Like When You Guys Are Back Together Again.

"So, this friendship thing . . ." he began. Then he looked out across the parking lot. The way he stared, you'd have thought he was taking in the most beautiful vista this side of the Grand Canyon, instead of a dozen cars and SUVs with only a row of bald trees between them and the road.

My heart was pounding. I could feel a light sheen of sweat break out over my whole body. "Yeah?" I said.

He shook his head at the horizon. "Kinda weird, isn't it?"

"Kinda," I said, thinking, *if by* weird *you mean earth-shatteringly horrible.*

He reached out suddenly and put his arm around my neck, pulling me toward him. I thought for a second that we were about to start making out, but then he just brushed his lips against the top of my head and released me.

The whole thing was over so fast it was almost like it didn't happen.

"Well, have a good weekend," he said. He didn't look at me when he said it, just stepped off the curb and onto the parking lot.

"Sure," I managed to say. "You too."

♥ ♥ ♥

I called Clara and Martha from the road.

"What does it *mean?*" I said, once I'd told them about the kiss.

"Maybe it means he wants to get back together," said Martha. I wished we were in the same room instead of on the phones in our respective cars; I wanted to throw my arms around her and tell her I loved her.

"Or maybe it means he's a complete loser," said Clara; I did *not* want to throw my arms around Clara (unless it was to strangle her).

"Why?" asked Martha. "Why is he a loser?"

"Because if he wants to get back together he should just *say* he wants to get back together."

"Maybe he's afraid I'll be mad at him," I said.

"You mean on account of his being a total loser?" said Clara.

I ignored her question. "Do you think he thinks he made a mistake?" I asked. I hoped Martha would answer, not Clara.

"It *definitely* seems that way," said Martha.

Clara sighed but refrained from saying anything. I was glad. After what Martha had just said, there was really nothing more I wanted to hear.

♥ ♥ ♥

My dad and Jay have a beautiful loft in Tribeca, all blond

wood and supermodern furniture—just the kind of place you'd expect a designer and his boyfriend to live. Before they bought their current apartment, they lived in Chelsea, but then—according to Jay—they got tired of being "the gayest cliché ever" and decided to move farther downtown. Sometimes we'll be out for dinner in their neighborhood and I'll point out that they're not exactly the only gay couple for miles, which makes Jay say they might have to move to Indiana or even, God forbid, The Upper East Side.

I'd planned to ask them about their trip to China before launching into the whole Max saga, but after what happened in the parking lot, I couldn't bring myself to wait. I'd barely made it across the threshold of their apartment before the story came spilling out of me.

"Oh, sweetheart, I am so, so sorry," said my dad when I'd more or less finished telling him what had happened. He was sitting next to me on the couch and Jay was sitting on the coffee table, facing us. "I'm so sorry you have to go through this."

"Dad, I need *advice*, not sympathy." I'd been counting on my dad and Jay to give me a guy's perspective.

"Oh, God," said my dad, rubbing his forehead, "I'm the worst at this stuff."

"Jay?"

Jay went over to the bar and started making me a Sunny-side Up, which is this special "cocktail" he invented for me a few years ago. It's ginger beer and seltzer with a splash of cranberry juice and a wedge of lime. While he sliced the lime he said, "Well, the bad news is, it doesn't look good."

My stomach sank. This was definitely *not* what I wanted to hear. Before I could ask him why he thought that, he said, "But the *good* news is, when you're ready, I have the perfect guy for you."

I tried to laugh, but it came out more like a bark. The idea that I'd let my dad and Jay fix me up with someone was simultaneously hilarious and horrifying— like letting Nana dress me for an important event. Last spring, before I was going out with Max, Jay and my dad came to this awards banquet at Hillsdale, and after the ceremony they *both* told me they thought I should go out with Scooter Prescott, who, in addition to being *two years* younger than I am, is possibly the hugest dweeb at Hillsdale.

"No offense, Jay," I said as he handed me the drink, "but I don't think we have the same taste in guys."

"What are you talking about? I have *wonderful* taste in guys." He sat down again on the coffee table again. "Look at your father."

I took a sip of my drink. It was perfect—slightly

sweet, slightly spicy. "Okay, Jay, that's like, completely gross."

"Sorry," he said. "But seriously, this one's a keeper. I've known him since he was born, he's completely adorable, and he writes for his school paper. Can you spell happily ever after?"

My dad furrowed his brow for a minute. Then he must have realized who Jay was talking about because he got a *Eureka!* look on his face and said, "I know, Eugene Barry?"

I laughed so hard some of my drink came out my nose. "Eugene!" I said when I could talk again. "You want to fix me up with someone named *Eugene*?! Why don't you just fix me up with someone named Dork!"

Jay raised his eyebrows at me. "Well, we can't all have snappy names like Mr. Fabulous Max Brown, now, can we?"

I was glad we were back on the subject of Max, since there was a serious question I needed to ask. "Do you think I was an overbearing girlfriend? Because I know I can be kind of bossy, and maybe I was being like that with Max, and maybe that's why he broke up with me."

Shaking his head, Jay went back to the bar and started mixing himself a gin martini, which he says is the only civilized thing to drink besides Evian. "Sweetheart, this is not a road you want to go down. Trust me. You're just going to tie yourself up in knots."

"But do you think he *might* want to get back together? I mean, based on everything I've told you."

"'Only the Shadow knows,'" said Jay, which is this line from some old radio show that my dad and Jay use whenever they don't want to answer a question. It's completely annoying, but tonight I didn't push my line of questioning. Jay's "It doesn't look good" had put a big dent in the shiny new happy-mobile I'd been riding around in ever since Martha said it seemed like Max might want to get back together.

Clearly he was not the right person for me to discuss the situation with. Instead, I asked them about China, and we spent the rest of the evening talking bamboo.

EIGHT

• • •

LET'S THINK ABOUT ALL THE THINGS WE HAVE TO BE GRATEFUL FOR

MAX DIDN'T CALL ME ALL WEEKEND. Sunday night, when my mom and Danny and I were eating dinner, the phone rang, and I jumped up to get it so fast Danny said, "Chill, babe. Chill."

I flipped him the bird and grabbed the phone. "Hello?"

"Karen?" It was an unfamiliar male voice; my heart sank.

"No, sorry, this is Jennifer. I'll get her." I was about to hand my mom the phone, when the expression on her face made me remember I'd forgotten something. I put the receiver back to my ear. "May I ask who's calling?"

"Oh, sure. Sorry, I should have said hello to you,

Jennifer. This is Evan Green. My son's on your brother's hockey team. We met at the hospital last week." A vague memory of a man with glasses rose up through the miasma of my disappointment at his not being Max.

"Yeah, sure," I said. "I remember you. Hang on a sec."

I held the phone out to my mom and said in a formal voice, "Dr. Green calling for Karen Lewis."

My mom wiped the corner of her mouth before taking the phone from me. "Hi, Evan," she said. And then, without waiting for him to say anything, she said, "We're just finishing up dinner. Can I call you back?" She listened for a minute before nodding and saying, "Great. I will." Then she hung up.

"Man, that dude's *desperate*," Danny observed, swirling some pasta onto his fork. "What is his *problem*?"

"What are you talking about?"

Danny opened his mouth to answer me, but my mom shut him down. "We do not speak with our mouths full, Daniel," she said. Normally I find my mom's saying stuff like that completely annoying, but the eyeful of half-masticated pasta I'd just gotten made me say a silent *Amen* for table manners.

Danny made a big show of swallowing what was in his mouth before taking a drink of water and then opening wide to show us just how not-full his mouth was.

Even without the food, the sight wasn't the most appetizing I'd seen.

"That Dr. Green loser," he said. "Totally jonesing for Mom."

"Seriously?" I asked, looking from my mom to Danny.

"Seriously," Danny said.

"Mom, would you care to comment?" I asked.

She shrugged and took a sip of wine. "Your brother's account of his pursuit is highly exaggerated," she said. "He's called a couple of times."

"At the game," Danny said, leaning toward me, "he was all . . ." Danny raised and lowered his eyebrows at me in a hilarious imitation of a guy coming on to a woman. "'Well, *hello*, there, Karen. You're looking *lovely* in that fashionable down parka of yours.'"

My mom threw a napkin at him. "You're impossible, you know that?"

"Manners, Mother," said Danny, waving his finger at her. "Manners." He stood up and (minor miracle) walked his plate over to the dishwasher. "Seriously, though. Dr. Green is no stud like yours truly, but he's a catch. And let's face it—you're not getting any younger. I say, strike while the iron man's hot."

"Danny!" I shouted. "That is so mean."

He raised his hands in a gesture of innocence. "I didn't say she's a *dog* or anything," he said.

"Thanks, Dan," said my mom. "I'll take that as a compliment."

Danny crossed his arms and looked mom up and down, like he was a judge on *America's Next Top Model*. "You're okay," he said. "You know, for a mom."

She stood up. "Really, you're too kind," she said, walking over and hugging him.

"*MOM!*" He wiggled out of her embrace. "Don't mess with the D-man."

My mother looked at the clock. "Well, the D-man better get cracking on his H-work or he's going to be in B-trouble."

"Uh, Mom?" said Danny, putting his hand on her arm. "You're okay-looking and everything, but try not to act cool, okay?"

"Upstairs!" she bellowed, pointing at the ceiling.

It was weird to imagine some guy being all crushed out on my mother. Did he think about her when she wasn't around the way I think about Max, and Martha thinks about Todd?

Ah, *gross.*

I brought the serving bowl over to the counter, trying to keep my voice casual. "So, um, are you . . . you know, are you going to go out with this guy?"

"Oh . . ." She waved vaguely. "No. All that's behind me, thank God."

I assumed that by "all that," she meant not only Evan Green but men in general. Since I wasn't exactly dying to hear yet again the many reasons "all that" was behind her, I said I had homework to do and headed up to my room.

Halfway up the stairs I realized I'd left my backpack under the table. I went downstairs to retrieve it, and when I got to the kitchen, I saw that my mom was standing exactly where I'd left her, Saran Wrap in one hand, half-full bowl of pasta puttanesca sitting uncovered in front of her on the counter.

"Mom?"

"Hmm?" She was staring out the window at, as far as I could tell, nothing.

"Mom?" I said again.

She turned to me quickly, like I'd woken her. "Yeah?"

I looked at her carefully. "Are you okay?"

"I'm fine, sweetheart." As if to prove just how fine she was, she pulled a long sheet of Saran Wrap from the roll, zipped it off, and began vigorously pinching it around the edge of the bowl.

"Okay," I said. "Well, see you later."

"Sure, honey," she said briskly. "See you later."

♥ ♥ ♥

It was hard not to feel depressed Monday morning about the fact that, when you got right down to it, all my hopes for a reconciliation with Max currently hung on the fact that he'd zipped up my jacket for me three days ago. I was so preoccupied with feeling sorry for myself and my TABLE FOR ONE, that when Martha ran up to me in the hall between first and second period and said, "My fifth period class was canceled," I didn't immediately put two and two together.

"So you have to go out for coffee with me," she concluded, walking alongside me even though her class was in the opposite direction. "It's fate that my class was canceled right when you have a free period."

The instant Martha uttered the word "fate," it was like a bolt of lightning went off in my brain: Martha's class had been canceled when I had a free. Her class had been canceled when I had a free *and* a meeting with Todd!

A diabolical plan immediately crystalized.

"Um, I have to do some stuff for the *Spectator*," I said. That much was true enough, but I crossed my fingers behind my back in anticipation of the whopper that was about to come out of my mouth.

"Can't you blow it off?" she asked.

"I wish," I lied. Then I paused, hoping my face looked like it would look if I'd suddenly, right that second, had an idea. "Hey, would you mind doing me a favor?"

Asking Martha if she'll do you a favor is a completely

rhetorical exercise since she's pretty much the most generous person in the universe. I swear, if she were on *Survivor*, she'd just vote herself off the island to help the other contestants win.

"Sure," she said.

"I'm *insanely* busy with production today, and I don't have time for lunch. Do you think you could get me a sandwich at the deli and bring it by the *Spectator* office fifth period?"

We were walking, so she couldn't see my face, but my voice sounded so obviously fake I totally expected her to go, *Okay, Lewis, what's really going on?* But either Martha's more gullible than I realized or I'm a better actress than I think I am, because she just asked me what kind of sandwich I wanted and then went off to class, so trusting I almost called her back and told her the truth.

Almost.

♥ ♥ ♥

Fifth period Todd was waiting for me in the empty *Spectator* office. I pulled out the chair next to his and dropped my bag on the ground.

"I'll show you mine if you show me yours," I said, sliding my questions over to him.

When we'd talked Friday, Todd and I had agreed that his questions would focus on black students and mine would focus on white students. He handed me his list of questions.

1. Is there a black community at Hillsdale? If so, do you consider yourself part of that community?

2. Define segregation. Do you think segregation exists at Hillsdale?

3. How often are you the only black student in a class? What is that experience like for you?

4. Do you take any classes in which there are few or no white students? If so, what kinds of classes are these (i.e., honors, inclusion, etc.)?

5. When you see African American adults at school, what jobs are they performing (i.e., administrative, custodial, etc.)?

6. Do you play on a team? If so, what percentage of your team is not white?

7. Do you socialize primarily with black or white students?

8. Is your neighborhood primarily white or black, or is it integrated?

97

I looked up at Todd. "These are good," I said.

"Yours are too," he said and slid them back to me.

1. Would your friends or parents care if you went out with someone who was African American?

2. Do you have friends who are African American?

3. Do you imitate rappers and/or call your friends "my homey" or "my nigga"?

4. Do you ever tell jokes or make comments you wouldn't make if an African American person could overhear them?

5. Do you take honors classes? If so, are there any African American students in your classes?

6. Do you have any African American neighbors?

7. Have you read a book for English this year that wasn't by a white author?

"The thing about your second one," said Todd, pointing to it, "is the answer could give the wrong idea. Like, all of my white friends would say yes, but they'd all be talking about the same person. It's not like they're hanging out with a bunch of black kids."

"Good point," I agreed. I took out a pen and changed it to, *Are most of your friends the same race as you?* Rereading our other questions and trying to see if they had the potential to result in misleading answers, I realized something I'd never noticed before. Moving my pen from number six on my list to number eight on Todd's, I said, "This is kind of about money, you know?"

Todd looked down at the question my pen was on and nodded. "Yeah, it's definitely a class thing, not just a race thing." He pointed at himself. "Exhibit A."

Todd was right—he was a perfect example of how racial issues in Hillsdale were also class issues. Todd was one of about a dozen rich black kids at Hillsdale High, and all of them were in honors classes, hung out with white kids, and ended up at Ivy League schools. I thought about the cafeteria and its all-black tables, where the guys wore stocking caps and jewelry and the girls had complex, elaborate hairstyles and long, brightly colored nails. If a black student was sitting at a table with white students, he was always conservatively dressed, like Todd, in jeans and a collared shirt, with maybe a Banana or Abercrombie suede jacket slung over the back of his chair (probably carrying the keys to his BMW or Lexus in the pocket).

Todd pointed at my first question. "Like, with this

one about dating someone of a different race." I held my breath, thinking of Martha and hoping he wouldn't say, *I'd never date someone who wasn't black.* "My friends would be way less freaked out by my dating a rich, Princeton-bound white girl than they would if I suddenly started showing up at parties with some girl from the Avenues." The Avenues is the part of Hillsdale where most of the black and Latino students live.

It was tempting to follow up what Todd had just said, but this didn't seem an opportune moment to ask, *So, did you have any particular Princeton-bound white girl in mind?*

I thought about the differences between Todd's neighborhood and the Avenues. "If we're going to talk about class, we're basically asking people how much money their parents make. That's going to be weird," I said.

"Not if we do an anonymous survey," Todd said. "I could ask my math teacher how you do a survey, you know, like what's a representative sampling and stuff."

"You mean survey the whole school?"

He shrugged and nodded, like it was no big deal. "Yeah, then maybe do a few in-depth follow-up interviews."

"Wow," I said, tucking my hair behind my ear. "I won't lie to you—that kind of freaks me out." I'd never done anything on such a big scale before.

Todd smiled. "Me too," he said.

I reread the questions, which made some of my confidence come back; they were good. Half thinking out loud, I said, "This is really different from what the *Spectator* normally does, isn't it?"

I hadn't meant anything by that, but then Todd muttered, "Thank God."

I looked up at him, surprised by how frustrated he sounded. "What do you mean?"

Todd gave me an I-think-you-know-what-I'm-talking-about look. "I just don't think the paper's all that interesting. I mean, the kids at Hillsdale who are interested in who's running for Senate, they're not getting their news from the *Spectator*. They're all like Andrew Murphy." (Andrew Murphy, in addition to wearing a suit to school every day, is never seen without a copy of the *Wall Street Journal* or the *New York Times* in hand.)

I thought about how Max had countered my arguments when I'd brought up the concerns Todd was voicing. "Don't you think it's our responsibility to help other kids get *into* stuff like politics? You know, get informed about what's happening outside our little universe?"

Todd shook his head. "An article like this one"—he pointed at the questions in front of us—"is *way* more important than all that other so-called political stuff we

101

write. And if *you're* editor in chief next year, I hope you'll think about that."

Thinking about being editor in chief gave me the shivers, but it seemed cocky to respond like I was sure that next year's paper was already mine. Instead, I gave Todd my most serious look, as if I were about to deliver a deeply significant response to what he'd just said. "You're saying we need a gossip column, aren't you?"

Todd laughed. "Oh, definitely," he said.

Right at that moment the door swung open, and Martha burst in with a brown paper bag from the deli in front of her face.

"One tuna-on-whole-wheat-hold-the-lettuce coming right up," she shouted like a town crier. Then she lowered the bag and saw Todd, and for a second I thought she was about to become a very different kind of crier.

"Hi there," he said, and the smile he gave her was nothing like the ones he'd been giving me. "You got anything in that bag for me?"

"No, I, ah, didn't realize you'd be here," said Martha. She looked at Todd for a second, then dropped her eyes.

"Hey, I was just kidding," he said. Nobody spoke for a minute, and I wondered if this was what people meant when they said, *It seemed like a good idea at the time.*

Todd pushed his chair back. "I'll talk to Mr. Connolly about how we structure and compute a survey."

"Sure," I said. "I'll tell Barton the plan."

"Great," said Todd. Then there was a long pause as both of us realized there really wasn't anything left for us to discuss. Suddenly I was in a panic. Was he just going to *leave?*

"Um, I have to go," I said quickly. "I have to find Mr. Barton. He's . . . um . . . having a root canal at two. Well, see you guys."

Mine wasn't exactly the smoothest dismount in the history of romance, but at least I got out of there (even if I did have to abandon my sandwich).

♥ ♥ ♥

Martha didn't answer either of the text messages Clara and I sent her, so we had to wait until the end of the day—two entire periods—to find out what had happened with her and Todd. When the bell rang at two forty-five, I practically sprinted to my locker. Clara must have run, too, because when I got there she was already waiting.

Martha was nowhere in sight.

"He *has* to have asked her out," I said, leaning back against my locker. "You don't understand the way he was looking at her."

"Show me," said Clara.

I lowered my lids and stared at her. "Hey there," I said in a deep, sexy voice, "I'm completely in love with you." We both cracked up.

The hallway started emptying out. Even though her history class *was* at the other end of the building, objectively, Martha should have shown up already. Had her teacher kept the class late? Or was something else going on? What if after I'd made it completely obvious that he was supposed to ask her out, Todd had just said, *Well, nice seeing you again. Bye.* What if he had a girlfriend at another school? What if right this second Martha was sitting in some bathroom crying her eyes out? What if—

"Will you stop doing that," Clara snapped, grabbing my wrist. "You're making me nervous." I hadn't even realized I was impatiently drumming my hands against my thighs.

"Well, I'm about to be late to the *Spectator* meeting," I snapped back, too freaked by the scenarios materializing in my brain (*Martha inconsolable. Martha weeping, "You ruined my life, Jennifer! Everything was fine until you got involved."*) to speak them.

And I *did* want to get to the meeting. I'd found Mr. Barton and told him about the idea Todd and I had for surveying the whole school on race relations, and he'd said he'd tell Mr. Michaels, the principal, what we were planning. I was dying to talk to the rest of the board about the article, but no way was I leaving until I knew what had happened with Todd and Martha.

I looked at my watch. "Do you think she—" but I didn't get to finish my sentence because suddenly there was Martha coming down the hall.

We ran to meet her. "What happened?" asked Clara.

"What did he say?" I asked at the same time.

Martha's cheeks were flushed, and a few strands of hair had come loose from her ponytail and were floating gently around her face. She looked beautiful, like a Renaissance painter had imagined her and then brought her to life.

If Todd hadn't asked her out, he was a total idiot.

She covered her face with her hands and shook her head.

"What?" I said, beyond nervous now. I put my arm around her shoulder and squeezed, simultaneously hating Todd for whatever he'd done and hoping *she* didn't hate *me* for the same reason.

"Did something bad happen?" asked Clara.

Martha dropped her hands to her sides and looked at us, her face a picture of complete bewilderment. "He just . . . asked me out." She shook her head, like she couldn't believe the words she'd spoken.

"He *did*?!" Relief washed over me.

She walked to her locker slowly, like someone coming out of a dream. Clara and I followed her. "Mmm hmm," she said.

"What did he *say?*" asked Clara.

Her forehead against the metal, Martha looked at us out of the corner of her eye. "He said, 'You want to go out sometime?' and I said, 'Yeah,' and he said, 'How about this weekend?' and I said, 'Sure.'" She closed her eyes and smiled. "And then he told me to call him."

"Wait," said Clara, taking Martha by the shoulders and turning her around. "He told *you* to call *him?* Why couldn't *he* call *you?*"

"Clara, I thought you're supposed to be a feminist," I said. "What's wrong with a girl calling a guy?"

"Nothing," said Clara. "Except this isn't a girl calling a guy. It's a guy *telling a girl* to call a guy."

Martha waved her hands in front of our faces. "Um, hello, could we please have a truce here?" She held out her cell phone. "I mean *right there.* He told me to call him so he'd have my number, okay?" Flipping her phone open, she mimed dialing a number into it, then held it up to her ear.

"Oh," Clara said.

"Oh," I said.

Martha still had the phone pressed up to her ear. "When his phone rang he answered it," she said, practically sighing at the memory. "And he said, 'Hello?' And I said, 'Hello?'"

Her story made me remember my first phone call with Max as we stood in the hallway. How did people get together before cell phones?

Martha continued. "And he said, 'Hey, I'm glad you called. You want to see a movie Friday?'"

I screamed. So did Clara.

"So wait, you said yes, right?" said Clara.

Martha nodded. "I said, 'That sounds like fun.'" For the first time since she'd started telling the story, Martha frowned. "I know that was lame. I should have said something wittier, but I couldn't think of anything."

Clara laughed. "Martha," she said, "it's fine. He *likes* you."

Martha turned to me. "He does, doesn't he?"

"Yeah," I said quietly. "He does."

♥ ♥ ♥

Everyone was already at the meeting when I got there, and both chairs next to Max were taken, one by Mr. Barton, the other by Anya. As I pushed open the door, a cell phone started ringing. It rang three times before Anya said, "Ohmygod, that's me!" and started frantically digging through her enormous, embroidered bag. She fumbled around with the buttons for at least two more rings before saying "Aha!" triumphantly and setting it down on the table. Max shot her a look like, *Could you please try to be a little less of a fruitcake?* Then he saw me standing there and his expression changed ever so slightly. I couldn't put my finger on exactly how, but I figured any change from how he looked at Anya had to be a good thing.

Todd and I gave each other a little wave hello. I wondered if he knew that I knew about him and Martha. I wished there were some way I could communicate my approval, but giving him a big thumbs-up seemed about as lame as it was possible to be without actually being someone's mom.

"Before we get started," Mr. Barton said, "I want to let the board know that after a conversation Ms. Lewis and I had this afternoon, I spoke with Mr. Michaels. In response to her and Mr. Kincaid's suggestion that the paper conduct a survey on race relations at Hillsdale, Mr. Michaels said no."

"What?" Todd and I looked at each other, shocked.

"Wait, I don't know anything about this," said Max, looking from me to Todd to Mr. Barton in confusion.

Mr. Barton explained. "Ms. Lewis and Mr. Kincaid are interested in writing an article about race at Hillsdale. In order to write said article, they felt it would be a good idea to find out how Hillsdale students feel about the subject. This is where Mr. Michaels comes in. He feels, and I quote, 'It would create racial tensions at Hillsdale where there currently are none.'"

"That is *such* crap," said Todd, slamming the table for emphasis. "He means it will look bad for the school if we admit there are racial issues here."

"Perhaps," Mr. Barton said, his voice even. "Perhaps. The question is, what is this board's response?"

"Let's do the survey anyway," said Todd. "It's not like he's going to physically prevent us from handing out surveys to the student body."

"Technically, he could suspend you," Max pointed out. "He could suspend all of us if he wanted to. *And* he could refuse to let the article run. The administration is allowed to do that."

Todd pursed his lips like he was about to say something, then didn't.

"What do you think we should do?" I asked Mr. Barton.

"As the *adviser* to the *Spectator*, I can only *advise*," said Mr. Barton, leaning back in his chair and folding his hands over his stomach. "I therefore suggest you decide what you want to do and then ask my advice about it."

"I say we do the survey anyway," said Todd again. "Show Michaels he can't censor the paper just to keep some bogus image of the school out there."

"Look, Todd," said Max, "maybe Mr. Michaels is right. Maybe it will create tensions that don't exist."

"The tensions exist," said Todd firmly.

Max tried a different tack. "Okay, maybe they do. But is that a story? And even if it is," he added quickly, "is it a story worth getting *disciplined* for?" I couldn't stop a disloyal thought—that Max was against the article just because he hadn't come up with the idea—from flickering across my brain.

"I think this *is* worth getting disciplined for," said Todd. "And if your personal goals for graduation conflict with what's in the best interests of this paper, maybe you should think about how to address that particular conflict of interests."

We all knew what Todd was referring to. At Hillsdale, the valedictorian isn't just the person with the highest grade point average. The valedictorian is the senior who has both a high grade point average (though not necessarily the highest) and who also meets certain criteria, like contributing to the school and being respected by teachers and stuff like that. It's a pretty big deal, and everyone knew Max had a good chance of being picked.

Instead of defending his personal goals for graduation, Max went on the offensive. "So now you're the expert on what the best interests of the paper are?" he asked.

"I'm saying this is the first *real* story we've considered covering all year. I'm saying if we walk away from this to write about some global warming summit that's going to be ancient history by the time the next issue comes out, we don't deserve to call ourselves journalists."

"I think you're being a little dramatic," said Max. "This isn't exactly the Pentagon Papers."

I knew the Pentagon Papers had something to do with the Vietnam War, but I wasn't exactly sure what they were.

"It's a hell of a lot closer than anything else we've done," said Todd. Then he crossed his arms and sat back in his chair, his lips a tight line of annoyance.

Todd and Max fighting was starting to really freak me out. If Max and I did get back together, how were the four of us going to share a limo on prom night if Todd and Max weren't speaking?

I cleared my throat to talk just as Anya said, "It's not exactly breaking news that the administration's a bunch of douche bags." Max looked over at her like he wished Hallmark made a card that said, *Thanks for your totally inarticulate defense of my position.*

"Maybe there's another way we could do the article," I said into the silence that Anya's comment had engendered.

"Pray continue, Lewis," said Mr. Barton.

"Well, what if we did an article about the administration's refusing to let us do the survey. We could interview Mr. Michaels and let him explain his position."

Mr. Barton raised his eyebrows. "You're devious, Lewis," he said.

Todd said, "I like it. Let them hoist themselves on their own petard."

"Nothing like going into a story without bias," said Max, but he was smiling, too. "So, I guess that's your story, J-Lo." He hadn't called me that since our breakup. The combination of Max's calling me by my old nickname and everyone else looking at me like I'd just turned water into wine gave me the sensation that if I wanted to, I could float up to the ceiling and fly around the room.

When the meeting ended, Max brushed me lightly on the shoulder as he left. I stayed behind to talk to Mr. Barton about my nonexistent internship application essay, trying not to be bummed about Max having left without following up on the J-Lo thing.

After I'd assured Mr. Barton that my ideas for the essay were definitely "percolating" (whatever that was), I met Clara and Martha in the student lounge. As we walked to the parking lot, Clara asked if I wanted to go to a movie Friday night.

"Sure, Clara," I said brightly. "Do you think Martha wants to come with us to the movies?"

"I don't know," Clara said, equally brightly. "Should we ask her?"

"Guys, quit it," said Martha, who had turned beet red.

"Hey, Martha," I said, my voice singsongy. "You want to go to a movie with us Friday night."

"Guys," said Martha.

"I get the feeling she might have *other plans*," I said to Clara. "But what could they be?"

"Gosh, Jenny, I just can't imagine."

"Come on, now. Quit it," said Martha.

"Quit what?"

We were at her car now, and she waved the keys threateningly. "Don't make me make you walk home."

But as soon as she'd pulled out of the parking lot, I couldn't resist saying, "If Martha's got plans Friday, do you think we could join her?"

"That's a great idea," Clara said. "I mean, she couldn't *not* want *us* to come, right?"

"Of course not," I said.

"You're hilarious," said Martha. "You two should take this on the road."

"Actually," said Clara, with a gesture that took in the car, the street, and the scenery, "we *are* on the road."

Sometimes when the three of us start laughing, it feels like we'll never be able to stop.

NINE

. . .

Do What You Love to Do—
With *You*!

Since Todd and Martha went to the movie theater at the mall, Clara and I couldn't. Because can you imagine trying to comport yourself on a date while your two best friends are right there, eating popcorn a few aisles (or even a few theaters) away? Talk about stroke central. And anyway, in a crazy coincidence, *All the President's Men* was playing at the art theater in town, which (at the time, before the night's myriad ironies had revealed themselves) seemed like a dream come true; I had never seen my favorite movie on the big screen, and Clara had never seen it at all. First we planned on seeing the eight o'clock, but then Clara was late and I was starving, so we decided we'd get some Chinese food next door and see the ten thirty.

We spent almost the whole dinner talking about

Todd and Martha, wondering what they were doing, what movie they'd gone to, if she'd call us with an update if he went to the bathroom or something. Then Clara dared me to call Martha and *ask* what they were doing, then I dared Clara to text her. In the end we were incredibly mature and didn't bother her once, which should go down as some kind of *world record*.

I wanted to just be happy for Martha and Todd, but I couldn't help thinking about Max and wondering where he was tonight. The fact that the restaurant was practically wallpapered with red hearts in anticipation of February 14th, which was only three days away, didn't exactly help keep my mind off Max.

"I hate Valentine's Day," I said. I poked my complimentary pineapple chunk with a toothpick. "They should kill whoever came up with this holiday."

"They *did*," said Clara.

This was news to me. Had a mob of angry dumpees marched on Hallmark headquarters, ripping from limb to unfeeling limb the evil marketing genius who'd come up with the holiday?

"They *did*?"

"Saint Valentine," said Clara. She handed me one of the fortune cookies and ripped hers open. "He was martyred in, like, the Middle Ages or something."

"Oh," I said. "Well, he deserved it."

"No doubt," Clara agreed. Then she read aloud from the slip of paper she'd taken from her cookie. "You are a kind friend in times of trouble." She rolled her eyes up to the ceiling and tossed the scrap on the table. "That's not a fortune, it's, like, a character assessment or something. Why don't they just say, 'You are good at math.'"

I put my hand on Clara's and looked deeply into her eyes. "Clara, you *are* a kind friend in times of trouble." We both started giggling. "Darling," I continued, "will you be my Valentine?"

"Oh, yes, darling," she said. Then she leaned across the table and air-kissed both my cheeks. "Mmwah! Mwah!" Some of the diners at nearby tables stared at us, but they quickly looked away when we stared back.

"Open yours," said Clara.

I looked down at the pale cookie in my hand. It's not like I thought I'd crack it open and the fortune would say, *Max is going to ask you to get back together with him*, but I hoped it would say something that would at least speak to the current situation. Maybe, *Someone you know will realize he has made a terrible mistake* or *Happiness is just around the corner (and so is your ex-boyfriend, who wants to reconcile)*. I mean, I don't actually believe in things like fortune cookies.

Except that I kind of do. What if Dr. Emerson wrote

fortunes in her spare time and mine said He's Moved On and So Should You!

"Um, hello," said Clara, flicking her napkin at my hand. "The movie's starting in an hour and it's all the way next door, so, you know, get to it."

I split open the cookie, which, despite my trying to be careful, shattered into a million little pieces. A sign? If so, I chose to ignore it because the fortune I got was so unbelievably perfect.

Winds of change are blowing your way.

"Oh my God," I said when I'd read it.

"What?" asked Clara eagerly.

I held the slip of paper out to her. "'*Winds of change are blowing your way*,'" she read. "Maybe it means, *You will soon get over that jerk Max Brown and find a better boyfriend*."

"Ha, ha," I said. "You realize the man you're calling a jerk just happens to be my future husband."

"Ha, ha," she said. "You realize the man you're calling your future husband just happens to be a jerk."

We paid for dinner and decided to kill the time before the movie with hot chocolate at Penny's Sweet Shop since it was completely freezing out. The whole time we were sitting there, I could practically hear the fortune rustling in my pocket.

The sad thing is, winds of change *were* blowing in

my direction, only they weren't the balmy breezes of requited love I fantasized about while sipping my spicy hot chocolate with mini marshmallows. Instead, these winds were actually a tornado that rips the roof off your house, shatters all the windows and leaves every one of your possessions ruined beyond recognition, while you huddle in the cellar, hoping to survive until the storm passes.

♥ ♥ ♥

Clara is very picky about where she sits during a movie. She won't sit too close because it gives her a headache, and she won't sit to the side because then the screen's apparently at a weird angle and everything gets flattened out. She's only happy sitting dead center and toward the back, which means when you go to a movie with her, you practically have to arrive at the theater the previous day. Then, when she's finally settled on the perfect seat, she spends the whole time before the movie starts worrying that someone really tall is going to sit directly in front of her.

We were, of course, the only people on line, since anyone who wants to see *All the President's Men* has had about thirty years to do so.

"You realize we're half an hour early for a movie that about five other people are going to be seeing tonight." It was hot in the lobby, but I didn't want to take off my coat since then I'd have to carry it around, which is even more annoying than feeling all hot and prickly inside your parka.

A middle-aged couple came and stood behind us. Clara raised her eyebrows meaningfully in their direction, then leaned over and whispered in my ear, "You can tell those people would have gone for our seats if they'd been first."

"You're mentally ill," I said, but she just nodded at me like, *Oh, I know what I'm talking about.*

"I'm bored," I said a few minutes later.

"You're, like, two years old, you know that? I should have brought a Barbie for you to play with." One of the ticket takers announced they were now seating for the ten o'clock showing of some French movie, and the couple that had been standing behind us went inside.

"It's annoying to stand in line," I said. "Especially when there's *no reason to do it*." I gestured to the now-empty lobby.

"Just wait," said Clara. "When the hordes arrive, you'll be glad I made you get here first."

I went and sat on the bench across the narrow lobby, leaning my head back against the frosted-glass mirror and thinking about Max. Where was he right now? Was he thinking about me the way I was thinking about him?

I closed my eyes and imagined him saying, *I missed you, Jennifer Lewis*. There was the rustle of coats and the whisper of a crowd of people coming through, and I realized the eight o'clock movie was letting out. I opened my eyes.

For a second, when I saw Max standing at the other end of the lobby, I thought my eyes were playing tricks on me. Actually, first I thought it was Max, then I thought it wasn't, then I recognized the jacket slung over his arm, a black parka with some old lift tickets still on the zipper, and I knew it was him.

I stood up, my heart pounding. This was it. *Winds of change are blowing your way*. Max had just walked out of my favorite movie in the world, alone. Could it *be* more obvious that he was thinking about me? I took a step in his direction just as he pushed back the sleeve of his sweater and looked at his watch. I had time to wonder why he was standing there, waiting for, as far as I could see, nothing. In that split second between his looking at his watch and my wondering what he was waiting for, I took another step toward him, and that's when I noticed he was standing a few feet away from, and looking at the door of, the women's bathroom.

The door to the bathroom opened, and Anya walked out. I stepped behind a life-size cardboard cutout of Rhett Butler carrying Scarlett O'Hara away from a flaming Tara as Anya walked over to Max. She was holding a single, long-stemmed rose. Max said something to her and they both laughed. Then he threw his arm around her shoulder before turning toward the exit.

Neither of them saw me. Anya's tousled hair must have blinded her because they'd only taken a couple of steps before she stumbled. I watched Max ask her a question, and she nodded, then tilted her face up to his. They kissed briefly. It wasn't an especially passionate kiss, but it definitely wasn't a friendly kiss. And it wasn't a first kiss either. It was the kind of kiss you give someone you've kissed before and know you're going to kiss again.

It was a couple kiss.

When Anya broke away from the kiss, she reached into her bag and dug around, finally extricating from its depths a hair clip. It was while she was holding the clip in her teeth and piling her hair onto her head that Max turned slightly toward the doors and saw me standing there, only partially obscured by Scarlett and Rhett.

His mouth dropped open, and he took a step in my direction. I don't know what would have happened next—if he would have come over to talk to me or if he would have kept standing there, staring, like I was some kind of horrible traffic accident he'd been unable to prevent—because suddenly Clara was at my elbow

saying, "Come on," leading me from the lobby and into the street. Though I have no recollection of our walk down the block, somehow we got to my car. Clara took my bag from me and dug the keys out, and then she was shutting the passenger door and sliding behind the wheel, peeling away from the curb even before she'd turned on the lights.

She kept looking at me, going, "Are you okay? Are you okay?" When I didn't answer her she said, "It's okay if you just want to scream or something."

But I was too shocked to scream. I was too shocked to do anything, too shocked to feel anything. Clara asked me if I wanted the heat on, and I realized my teeth were chattering with the cold. She leaned forward and adjusted the blowers, but even when the car had warmed up enough that I could no longer see our breath, I continued to shiver uncontrollably.

"Say something," said Clara when we'd stopped at a red light right before the turnoff to Meadow Lane. When I didn't respond, she turned to me. "Say something," she said again. "Anything."

I looked at her and saw the glint of other cars' headlights in her glasses, saw the neon of the pharmacy sign glowing behind her. Then I turned back to face the windshield.

"He is such an incredible asshole," she said. A car

behind us honked, and she made the left turn.

I knew I should say something in response, but I couldn't imagine what. I couldn't imagine why I would ever want to say anything again. I'd thought it was bad when Max broke up with me, but now I knew it wasn't. At least when he'd broken up with me, I'd been able to hope.

At least when he'd broken up with me, I'd been able to speak.

PART TWO

The Heartache

♥

TEN

• • •

THE MIRACLE THAT IS YOU

THE NEXT TWO DAYS UNFOLDED in the darkest, saddest place I'd ever been.

Martha and Clara and my mom came and went, bringing me ice cream and DVDs and books they said were guaranteed to make me laugh. My dad and Jay begged me to let them take me out to dinner, told me how wonderful I am and how much they love me. Even Danny tried to cheer me up with a rap he'd written about all the things of Max's that were mini *besides* his car.

But somehow I couldn't really respond the way I knew I was supposed to. I'd fake laugh at things that weren't meant to be funny, and I'd get sad and quiet when I was supposed to be laughing. Finally, whoever was there would leave, and for a second it was always

127

a huge relief, just being by myself and not having to pretend. But then I'd start to feel even worse than when I'd had company, so scared and alone I didn't think I could stand it for one more minute. So as big a relief as it was when they left, it was an even bigger relief when they came back bearing more ice cream, more movies; until the weight of their presence became unbearable to me again, and I found myself longing for them to go.

Sunday night my mother came into my room. I hadn't slept the past two nights so much as I'd lain in bed in a weird, hallucinatory haze that might have passed for some kind of rest if all of my hallucinations hadn't been so awful.

After forty-eight hours without sleep, everything was starting to get a little fuzzy around the edges.

"I want to talk about this," said my mom, sitting at my desk.

I assumed by "this" she meant Max and Anya, which was sort of weird since it seemed to me that was all we'd talked about for two days. What was there left to say? I said nothing.

"It has to be postmarked by tomorrow."

Oh. The *New York Times* application. Friday afternoon—a million years ago—I'd taken it downstairs to try to decide how to approach the essay. She must have found it on the kitchen table.

I would have said it was impossible to be any unhappier than I'd been a minute ago, but thinking about me sitting at the kitchen table, still hopeful about Max and looking forward to the summer and life in general, dropped me down into an even deeper, darker pit than the one I'd been occupying.

I still didn't have anything to say. If my mom thought I was going to write a three hundred and fifty word essay tonight, then she had some kind of secret crack addiction heretofore kept hidden from me.

"Honey, I know you're sad. Believe me. But that's no reason not to meet your responsibilities. Mr. Barton nominated you for this internship. You can't disappoint him."

I knew I was supposed to feel something when she said that. Mad, maybe, that she was trying to manipulate me? Ashamed by my irresponsibility? It was like I was looking through a closet of emotions, trying to figure out which one was appropriate for the occasion when really I felt nothing at all.

"Jenny?" She came and sat on my bed. I'd spent so much time all weekend bawling onto the shoulder of whoever was sitting next to me, it was kind of a Pavlovian response by now. My eyes welled up. She put her arm around me. "Oh, sweetheart." She pulled me close to her and kissed the top of my head, which only made me start crying for real. "Sweetheart, I really think it will make you feel better if you do this application."

I laughed. It might have been my first real laugh since Friday. "You don't understand, Mom. I *can't* do it."

My mom turned me to her by my shoulders and looked into my face. "Jennifer Lewis, how are you going to face Mr. Barton tomorrow if you haven't written this essay?"

Did my mother actually think I was going to go to school tomorrow? *Valentine's Day?* Talk about delusional.

"I'm not going to have to face Mr. Barton having not written this essay, because I'm not *going* to school tomorrow," I said. "Or Tuesday," I added, in case she hadn't figured it out.

"I don't want to fight with you, Jenny," she said. "Not when you're so sad."

"There's nothing to fight about."

"You're going to school and you're writing the essay."

"I'm *not* going to school. And I am *not* writing the essay."

My mom sighed. Or maybe it was one of those slow yoga breaths she usually reserves for the conversations she has with Danny about cleaning his room. Then she looked at me. Then she looked at the application in her hand. Then she looked back at me. Then, inexplicably, she smiled.

"All right, name your price."

"Excuse me?" That my mom had some kind of drug problem was seeming more and more likely.

She waved the application at me. "For this."

I looked at her. Was she serious? "You're going to *pay* me to write the application?"

"Not in money," she said. "In something else."

Suddenly I got where she was heading. In spite of myself, I smiled, too.

"One week," I said.

"Monday," she said.

"Four days."

"Two."

"Three."

"You can go in late on Wednesday."

"Deal."

♥ ♥ ♥

Since my mother hadn't made part of our deal any specific requirements regarding the *quality* of the application, I barely thought about what I wrote. Not that thinking would have helped. My brain was such a wasteland of sadness and confusion, *not* thinking probably helped. At the last second, I remembered to spell-check the essay, which was practically a miracle. I printed it up along with three articles that were "representative of my work" from the *Spectator*, filled out the application form, and gave it all to my mom in a manila envelope.

My get-out-of-jail-free pass.

♥ ♥ ♥

I actually managed to sleep Sunday night, which was kind of incredible. But anyone who says all you need is a good night's sleep to get over a problem obviously never had a real problem. Monday morning, instead of waking up exhausted and miserable, I just woke up well-rested and miserable. A huge box of chocolate arrived from my dad and Jay, but when I called to thank them, I had to admit I hadn't been able to eat any.

"I'm sorry, Daddy," I said, starting to cry once again. "It was really nice of you to send them."

"Oh, honey," he said, "I don't care about the chocolates. I just want you to be okay."

"I'm okay," I said, only, I was crying hard enough by then that it was pretty clear how okay I wasn't.

"No, you're not," he said. "But you will be. *I* know you will be even if you don't."

"Thanks, Daddy," I said, and then I didn't want to stay on the phone anymore, and he let me hang up.

♥ ♥ ♥

When I woke up Tuesday morning, I felt no better than I had Monday. Apparently I was now living proof that yet another platitude, *Time heals all wounds*, is total crap. I had absolutely no idea how I was supposedly going to function in school by eleven thirty the next day (the latest my mom had agreed to let me sign in). At this point, I was planning on just cutting my afternoon classes. What was she going to do, ground me? *Kill* me?

If only.

I was still in bed at noon when I heard a car pull into the driveway. I figured it was Clara and Martha, since they'd come by Monday at the same time. Yesterday, when Martha had said Todd hoped I'd get better soon, I'd tried to get her to tell me the details of her date, but Clara just said, "They had a great time, they're totally in love, we're not talking about it right now." Clearly she'd thought I was unable to handle the news that Martha had a boyfriend, but she couldn't have been more wrong. It was a relief to think about Todd and Martha; it kept me from thinking about Max and Anya. I'd managed to get through yesterday's visit without asking Clara and Martha if they'd seen them together, but I had the feeling that today I wasn't going to make it. The need to know was pressing on me, like something heavy that had taken up residence on my chest.

I stayed in bed and listened to the beeping of the alarm code being punched in. But the voice that called my name from the bottom of the stairs wasn't Clara's or Martha's.

"Jenny? Jennykins?"

I sat up. "Nana?"

"Jennifer, darling, where are you?"

"I'm upstairs, Nana."

I got out of bed and walked to the top of the stairs, almost bumping into Nana, who was just reaching the landing.

I don't know what I looked like (or smelled like, for that matter), but it can't have been pretty. I couldn't even remember the last time I'd showered, much less brushed my hair or changed my sweatshirt.

But Nana just put her arms around me and pressed her cheek against my (undoubtedly quite oily) head. "Oh, Jennykins. You poor darling." She sighed, and I wondered if she was thinking about Grandpa Harry. As we stood on the landing together, I couldn't help wishing that Max had died instead of dumping me for Anya. Then my sadness would have had something tragic and noble about it instead of just being plain old pathetic.

I was imagining myself at Max's funeral if he'd died while we were still going out, everyone whispering stuff like, *You know he was madly in love with her,* and *They would have been together forever if only that semi hadn't run him off the road*, when Nana stepped away from me so abruptly I swayed slightly.

"Now," she said, clapping her hands together. "I want you to take a shower."

"But, Nana, I——"

"'But, Nana, I,' nothing." She clapped again, twice. "Chop chop."

The truth was I was starting to disgust even myself, so I just nodded and went into the bathroom, where I took what might have been the longest, hottest shower in the history of indoor plumbing.

When I came out, Nana had opened the windows in my room and stripped the bed.

"Nana, it's *freezing* in here," I said, running in place while I grabbed clothes out of my drawers. I'd been planning on just getting back into pj's and crawling under the covers, but now that my room was arctic and my bed was bald, that option didn't look nearly so appealing. I pulled on a second sweater.

Nana was sitting at my desk reading a book. I wrapped my hair in a towel and brought my other towel and robe back to the bathroom. When she heard me come back in, she held up her hand to get my attention. "Listen to this," she said. "'There's no reason for you to keep feeling these things, you hot mama, you. What you need to feel is *powerful*. What you need to feel is *beautiful*. What you need to feel is the miracle of *you*'."

I couldn't believe this was happening. "Oh, Nana, please don't." I'd gotten a lifetime's worth of depressing "help" just from *The Breakup Bible*'s table of contents and introduction. The last thing I needed right now was for Nana to read the entire book out loud to me like it was the *actual* Bible.

Nana looked up from the page to me. "Do you hear that? *The miracle of you*. That's you, Jennykins. The miracle of Jennykins."

"Nana, the only miracle is that I'm still alive after the humiliation I endured on Friday."

Nana turned back to the book. "'So he's with somebody else,'" she read. "'Yeah, it hurts. Yeah, you miss him. But you know what? You're not going to miss him for long. Because if you follow my simple steps, you can go from heartache to happiness before you can say, *I'm over you!*'"

Nana was looking up at me, a triumphant expression on her face. "See?" she said. "You're not the only one."

"Nana, you don't understand," I said. "That book—" I pointed at it. "Books like that don't help." Had Nana not observed the obese hordes with their terrible hair and bad jeans crowding the self-help aisles at Barnes & Noble, reading books like *Who Moved My Destiny?* and *You're Not Weird, You're Special!*

"Just how do you know that, Miss Smartypants?" She pointed at me. "You won't even give it a chance." Then her features softened, and she smiled. "Give it a chance, darling. For me. For Nana." She stood up and walked over to where I was sitting. Then she put the book in my hand, folding my fingers over the spine. "Now, you get started on this while I make us something good to eat."

Just thinking about eating made me want to yak, but I didn't say that. And I didn't say anything about how it would be a cold day in hell before I turned to Dr. Emory Emerson for advice. Once Nana was downstairs I'd just put the book back on the shelf and forget all about it.

At the door, Nana turned back to me. "You're a good girl, Jenniline," she said. "You're good to your nana."

Oh, God, was I really going to lie to this woman? I felt my eyes welling up for the umpteen millionth time since Friday, but for a completely different reason. "Thanks, Nana," I said.

"You take your time," she said. "I'll be downstairs."

I nodded, too choked up to say anything.

Okay, first things first. I want you to take out a pen and write down your ex's top five faults—I know you'll probably have trouble stopping at five, but that's all we have room for right now ☺. Go on, use the space on this page, and write in BIG, BOLD letters.

Had there really been a time when I'd drawn a complete blank looking at this exercise? I grabbed a pen off my night table and started writing.

Liar—Pretended he cared if we were friends (really just didn't want me to be mad at him)

Cheater—Probably liked Anya even before we broke up (did something happen with them that night at his house after I left?!?)

Too chicken to tell me the REAL reason he wanted to break up

Let me believe he thought being friends was "weird" (i.e. that we might get back together)

Bad editor of the paper (only likes his own ideas)

Thinks he knows more about music than he really does

I realized too late that I had six, not five, so I drew an arrow from "Let me believe he thought being friends was 'weird'" to "Liar."

I can't say I felt better, but I definitely didn't feel worse, which was kind of a miracle considering every time I'd thought of Max over the past four days, I'd just wanted to crawl into a hole and die.

Nana called my name, and I walked downstairs, still reading the book. Chapter One was called, "Getting Over Mr. Wrong—or How I Learned to Stop Worrying and Love Myself."

I don't know about you, but it used to be that when some guy told me he didn't want to be my man anymore, my first thought was always, "Where did I go wrong?" I figured the fault had to be *mine* because otherwise why would someone as funny and smart and wonderful as the love of my life have dumped me? *I should be less demanding*, I'd think to myself. Or, *I'm not pretty enough*, or *Why was I always nagging him?* It never occurred to me that I could be the most wonderful woman in the world, and the man I (thought I) loved might still tell me to take a hike.

It's hard to read while walking down a flight of stairs.

But not impossible.

♥ ♥ ♥

Clara called and said she and Martha were inviting themselves over for dinner. Just after six o'clock, when they burst in the door, I was curled up on the little sofa in the kitchen (where I'd been all afternoon) with my new best friend: *The Breakup Bible*.

"What are you reading?" Clara asked. She lifted the book enough to read the title. "You're kidding me, right?"

Martha came over and squeezed in next to me. "Is it good?" she asked. "Is it helping?"

"I can't tell yet," I said, picking up my pen. Dr. Emerson wanted me to draw my feelings about the breakup. I drew a little rain cloud. Then I scribbled it out and drew a bigger rain cloud with a stick figure under it.

Clara stood behind the couch watching me draw. "Are you in some kind of cult?" she said finally.

I didn't even look up. "What, just because I'm doing something to make myself feel better, I'm in a cult? Are you on Team Jennifer or not?"

That's what Dr. Emerson called the people you were supposed to surround yourself with while you went through this time of healing and recovery: Team Jennifer. Well, she called it "Team _____" and then said, "insert your name here."

Clara tapped Martha on the shoulder and whispered, sotto voce, "She's in a cult."

I was about to respond, when the door opened and

my mother and Danny walked in. My mom's cheeks were pink from the cold, and she looked really pretty.

"Hi," she said, coming over and giving all three of us hugs. "It's so great to see you guys."

"Ladies, ladies," said Danny, nodding all around. Danny once confessed to me that he thinks Martha is a "total babe," and that Clara could be too, if she "worked it more," considering she has a "smokin' bod." My thirteen-year-old brother's critique of my best friends' "bods" is, to say the least, wildly revolting.

Everyone started talking, meaning I could just sit there not saying anything, which was fine with me. Only, when my mom walked over to the closet and took off her coat, I couldn't help noticing something.

"Hey, Mom, are those new jeans?" My mother usually wears *total* mom pants, like high-waisted corduroys from Land's End. But these looked like they were a pair of—

"Karen, are you wearing Diesel jeans?!" asked Clara.

My mom turned her upper body around, trying to read the label on the back. Clara stood up and went over to her.

"They *are* Diesel!" She pointed at the label on the front pocket.

"They look great, Karen," said Martha.

Danny, his mouth full, said, "They're for *Ev-an.*"

141

"Danny, that is completely untrue," my mom said. Her denial might have been more convincing if she hadn't been A) smiling, B) wearing lipstick (which she *never* does), and C) blushing.

"Who's *Evan?*" asked Clara and Martha in unison.

"He's nobody," said my mom. "Just a friend whose son plays on Danny's team. They had a practice today."

"Yeah, and we had to go out for *coffee* after, and his kid's a *total* dork." Crumbs flew around the room as Danny spoke.

"Daniel, please. Swallow your food before you speak. We are not animals."

"So do you *like* him?" asked Clara.

"He's very nice," said my mom, suddenly extremely busy wiping down the already sparkling clean counter.

"But do you *like* him?" asked Clara again.

I did mention that Clara plans to be a litigator, right?

"She *loooooves* him," said Danny.

My mother threw the sponge at Danny, who put up his hands in a gesture of innocence. "You all saw that, right?" he said. "That bitch *crazy.*"

"*Is* crazy, honey," said my mom. "That bitch *is* crazy."

♥ ♥ ♥

At first, I wasn't going to cut the inspirational messages out of *The Breakup Bible* and tape them up in my

142

me space, as per Dr. Emerson's instructions. First off, I felt like a total idiot doing it. And second, I was pretty sure my mom would have a conniption if she found me putting Scotch tape on the wallpaper in my room, since it's this special wallpaper from, like, a hundred years ago when our house was first built.

But then I thought about going to school tomorrow and seeing Max and Anya, and I started to panic. What if I froze up again, just like I did at the theater? Thinking of standing paralyzed in the two-hundreds corridor, unable to put one foot in front of the other, while my classmates circled around me like I was some kind of sideshow freak ("Step right up, ladies and gentlemen! Step right up and see the woman *paralyzed by the humiliation of being dumped!*") was all the motivation I needed to follow Dr. Emerson's instructions to the letter.

HE DIDN'T DESERVE ME!!! I AM BEAUTIFUL!!! MR. RIGHT IS RIGHT AROUND THE CORNER. MR. WRONG IS IN THE GARBAGE WHERE HE BELONGS. I COMPLETE ME!

My mother looked a little surprised when she came into my room and saw me taping DR. EMORY EMERSON'S TEN COMMANDMENTS to the full-length mirror on my closet door, but she didn't say anything about it, and she didn't say anything about the tape on the wallpaper, either.

"Hi," she said. She pushed aside the scraps, scissors, and tape scattered across my bed and sat down. "How are you doing?"

"I'm okay," I said, stepping back to see if the commandments were straight.

Dr. Emory Emerson's Ten Breakup Commandments

1. Move out
2. You cannot be friends
3. Do not process this breakup together
4. Do not bad-mouth your ex to other people
5. Get rid of anything that reminds you of him
6. Start an exercise regime
7. Pursue an interest you could not have pursued while you and your ex were together
8. Take a vacation
9. Embrace change
10. Go on a date—there are plenty of other fish in the sea

There was a certain amount of relief in knowing that, because obviously we'd never lived together, I'd already taken care of the first commandment—kind of like how on the SAT you supposedly get two hundred points just for writing your name. Of course that relief was lessened slightly by the knowledge that, equally effortlessly, I'd broken the second commandment. But that wasn't exactly my fault, was it? I mean, in order to have *not* broken it I would have had to somehow heard of, purchased, and read Dr. Emerson's book in the millisecond between Max's saying, "I think we should just be friends," and my saying, "Okay." Only then could I possibly have known that the correct response to Max's suggestion was, in fact, "No."

My mom cleared her throat. "I just want you to know that I'm really proud of you. I'm proud of how you wrote the essay and how you're going to school tomorrow. I know it's not easy."

Was she for real? "Uh, it's not exactly like I had a *choice*," I pointed out.

My mom didn't respond, just came over and stood next to me, reading the commandments. "These are . . . interesting." She pointed at number nine. "So, are you going to start job-searching?"

"It's not funny," I said sharply. Could she not see that stupid Dr. Emerson and her stupid book were all that stood between me and the abyss?

"I'm sorry, sweetheart," she said, squeezing me. "But you know, you don't need these. You're going to be just fine all on your own."

"Well, you'd certainly know about that, wouldn't

you?" I said. "You're kind of like the world's *expert* on being alone."

I knew from the look that flitted across my mom's face that I'd hurt her feelings, but I let her leave without saying I was sorry. Then of course, I felt terrible. Rereading Dr. Emerson's commandments, I added one of my own.

Try not to be a total bitch to everyone who loves you.

ELEVEN

. . .

GOING INTO SCHOOL LATE on Wednesday was possibly the worst idea in the brief history of Jennifer. Maybe if I'd arrived at the usual time with everyone else, I could have faked myself out, pretended life was getting back to normal. But walking alone down the deserted corridor from the office to my locker, my clicking heels the only noise in the near silent building, it felt like I was announcing my lonely, rejected freakdom to the world.

When I opened my locker, a tiny piece of folded paper fell out of it; I was so keyed up, I gave a tiny, involuntary scream, like the note was perhaps a bat or poisonous insect. My heart continued to pound as I stared at the spot on the floor where it had fallen. Was

147

it from Clara? From Martha? Or was it from . . . ? It wasn't until I bent down and started trying to open it that I realized my hands were shaking.

J-We NeeD to TaLK-M.

Even before I made out the words, seeing Max's handwriting was like taking a body blow. His letters are neat and blocky, a mix of capital and lowercase; I'd know his writing anywhere.

It was the "we" part of the note that really threw me. In math, while Mr. Leonard graphed parabolas on the board, I kept taking Max's note out of my wallet and rereading it. By the end of the period, the paper was so dog-eared it had started to rip along one of the folds. *We need to talk. We need to talk.* Not *I need to talk to you*, but *We need to talk.*

But *we* weren't a *we* anymore, were we? Wasn't he a *we* with Anya now? So what were *we* supposed to be talking about? *Us?* But there *was* no *us.* Just like there was no *we.* Only with no *us* and no *we*, *who* needed to talk?

And when, exactly, were *we* supposed to talk? At the next *Spectator* meeting? *Hi, Mr. Barton. Hi, Todd. Hi, everyone. Please excuse Max and me for a minute—we're just going to hash out our entire relationship for your listening pleasure.*

I wondered how Max and Anya had behaved at Monday's meeting. Now that they'd been outed, had they acted the way *Max and I* had acted in meetings—secret looks, footsie, private jokes? How dare Dr. Emerson call her book *The Definitive Guide to Breaking Up and Moving On* when she'd neglected to include crucial chapters like "How to Handle the Meeting of the School Newspaper's Board When You've Been Dumped for the New Contributing Editor"?

♥ ♥ ♥

When I got to my locker at lunch, Martha and Clara were waiting for me. I'd been half hoping, half fearing Max's being there, and when he wasn't, I felt simultaneously disappointed and relieved.

Martha opened her arms, and I more or less collapsed into them. Miraculously, I managed not to burst into tears as she hugged me.

"How'd re-entry go?" asked Clara.

"It went," I said.

They put their arms around me and we made our way down the hallway, pressed so tightly against one another you'd have thought we were fused at the hips.

"Oh," said Martha as we got to the exit. "Todd says he made an appointment for you guys to meet with Principal Michaels first period Friday."

I couldn't think that far ahead right now. Thinking about Friday meant thinking about the weekend, which meant thinking about all the days left in my life.

And how completely they were going to suck.

♥ ♥ ♥

You can actually do about ninety percent of a news-paper's production online, but when Mr. Barton sent me an e-mail saying he wanted to get some face time, I didn't think he'd find it funny if I just sent him a JPEG of myself. I was glad he named sixth period Thursday as a good time for me to meet him at the *Spectator* office, since I knew Max had a double lab period then and would never in a million years be there.

"Well, well, well," he said when I walked in the door. "Our long-lost managing editor."

I gave him a wan smile. I wasn't faking the wanness, either; just being in the *Spectator* room gave me the heebie-jeebies. "I was sick," I said.

Mr. Barton, apparently, was not as gullible as Martha. "And I'm the Queen of England," he said.

Oh, God, did Mr. Barton *know*? Was he going to want to talk about it? Was he going to want to *comfort* me? Just thinking about having to listen to Mr. Barton tell me everything was going to be okay made me want to run screaming from the room.

I don't know if he read my thoughts on my face or not, but all he said was, "Get your application in?"

"You bet," I said, flooded with relief.

"How'd it go?"

"Um, okay," I said, hoping my voice didn't convey my knowledge that I didn't have a snowball's chance in hell of getting the internship.

"No doubt you could have written it with half your brain tied behind your back," he said.

"Hey, that's how I wrote it," I said, and even though it was the first honest thing I'd said to him since I walked in the room, he laughed as if I'd just made a great joke.

"Well, I'm glad it's in," he said. He leaned back against his desk. "If you wanted to show me the questions you've prepared for your interview with Mr. Michaels tomorrow, I wouldn't say no. Mr. Kincaid's got an interesting angle."

My *prepared questions*? Mr. Barton had clearly confused me with a functioning human being. "Um, sure," I said. "I'll try to do that . . . later."

Mr. Barton pulled at his beard, giving me a sympathetic look. "I'm glad to see you back, Lewis."

Okay, that last comment was dangerously close to comforting. Blinking fast, I just said, "Thanks, Mr. Barton," and backed out the door.

Right into Max.

I don't know what the expression on my face was, but I can tell you how he looked: Stricken. *Stricken*. Really, you'd have thought *he* was the one who'd been dumped for Little Miss Can't Keep the Hair Out of Her Eyes.

The door to the office swung shut, leaving us standing alone in the hallway.

"I thought you had bio," I said automatically.

"Dr. Richmond's sick," said Max, equally automatically.

Once again, he was wearing the sweater we'd gotten together at Banana Republic, only this time at least I wasn't stupid enough to think it was some kind of special secret sign that he wanted to get back together.

I wrapped my fingers around the strap of my backpack as tightly as if it were a flotation device.

"Did you get my note?" asked Max. "I wanted to talk to you. I know you probably hate me, but——" he took a deep breath. "I hope you'll let me explain."

For a moment of what I can only describe as some kind of temporary insanity, I had the idea that by "explain" he meant *Explain what you saw the other night* as in *Explain how, even though it looks like Anya and I are a couple, you'll see that we aren't.*

Which goes a long way toward *explaining* why I said, "Fine."

Fine.

Not, *Why don't you go explain to someone who cares, since I so clearly don't.* Not, *Explain what?*

Fine.

He slid down the wall and put his backpack on his lap. Then he looked up at me. "You have every right to hate me," he said.

I shrugged.

"Look," he said, not looking at me. "I'm really, really sorry. I didn't mean for you to find out about me and Anya. I mean, I didn't mean for you to find out like *that*," he added quickly. "I was going to tell you. When I knew what was . . ." I waited while he figured out how to finish his sentence ". . . going on" is what he finally came up with. Then he added, "If you hadn't seen us Friday, I was going to tell you about it Monday. I want you to know that. I wasn't going to keep it from you anymore."

Suddenly I saw the wisdom in Dr. Emerson's third commandment. I mean, what about this conversation was supposed to be making me feel better? *When I thought it was just a fling, there was no point in telling you about us, but once it became clear we were completely in love, I wanted you to be the first to know.*

And what exactly was I supposed to say now?

Thanks for looking out for me.

I really appreciate your honesty.

Congratulations on your new relationship!

In lieu of any of these things, I just stood there,

staring down at him and thinking, *I'm so sad. I'm so sad. I'm so sad.*

Right then the bell rang. "I have to go," I said. I took a step away from him.

"Jen?" said Max, standing up.

"I really have to go," I said again, and this time I turned and started practically running toward English.

"Jenny?" he called after me. But the hallway was filling up with students, and I don't know if he tried catching up with me or not.

TWELVE

. . .

THE FOURTH COMMANDMENT: THOU SHALT NOT BAD-MOUTH THINE EX

First period Friday morning, Todd met me in the vestibule outside Mr. Michaels's office wearing a pair of khakis with an oxford under a really nice cashmere sweater. I'd dressed up a little, too, but not for the interview. Dr. Emerson says You have to put your best foot forward, and that foot, apparently, had to be well shod. Todd took in my knee-length gray skirt, black tights, and red turtleneck sweater and, clearly thinking we were both looking sharp for the same reason, gave me a knowing grin.

"Nervous?" he asked.

"A little," I admitted.

"Me too," he said.

I chose not to reveal to my fellow reporter that my

anxiety might have been heightened by the fact that I had absolutely no questions prepared. I hadn't even *thought* about what I was going to ask Mr. Michaels. During finals week, I sometimes have dreams where I'm in the middle of an exam for a class I haven't taken. This was kind of like that, only real life.

We sat for a minute; the only noise was the sound of Mr. Michaels's secretary typing away. I swear, she must have typed about a thousand words a minute.

"So, hey," said Todd. "I'm sorry about you and Max. That must really suck."

"Thanks," I said. And before I could stop myself I added, "He's just such an incredible asshole, you know?"

Too late, I remembered Dr. Emerson's fourth commandment; I wasn't supposed to be bad-mouthing Max to other people. Sometimes I wished Dr. Emerson's commandments weren't so hard to obey. Why couldn't she have taken a page from the Old Testament and commanded stuff like, "Thou shalt not kill thy ex or thy ex's idiot girlfriend"? I mean, that's the kind of commandment it's hard to break accidentally.

Luckily, Todd didn't seem to think less of me for having dissed Max to him. "Yeah, what he did was pretty lame."

Inspired by what I took to be his enthusiasm, I added, "Plus, Anya's a total retard."

Of course Mr. Michaels *would* choose *that* minute to

open his office door. "Miss Lewis. Mr. Kincaid. Won't you come in."

Had my referring to one of my fellow editors as a total retard compromised my position as a serious journalist in Mr. Michaels's eyes? Perhaps *this* was why Dr. Emerson suggested it might not be a good idea to badmouth one's ex. As Todd and I walked by him, I tried to read in Mr. Michaels's expression a reaction to what I'd said, but his face remained impassive.

"So," he said, sitting behind his desk and pressing his fingertips together. "You're here to interview me for the *Spectator*."

"Yes," said Todd. He took out his notebook and so did I, even though, unless Mr. Michaels spoke about ten words an hour, no way was I going to get down what he said. "We wanted to ask you about your decision not to approve the schoolwide survey on race relations at Hillsdale."

Right away, I could tell Mr. Michaels had *not* been anticipating this line of questioning; I guess he'd been expecting us to ask why they don't serve pizza more often in the cafeteria or why we can't have snow days even when it doesn't snow. He didn't *say* he objected to the subject of our interview, but he got that tight smile on his face authority figures get when underlings challenge them.

"As I believe I already told Mr. Barton," he said, "this is a nonissue." His message was crystal clear: *Drop it.*

I was way freaked out sitting there with Mr. Michaels clearly being pissed off at us. I mean, maybe he has a serious comb-over and drives a tacky sports car, but he *is* the principal. If it had been just me, I probably would have thanked him for his time, packed up my notebook, and run out of his office, grateful not to have been expelled.

But luckily, Todd wasn't as big a wimp as his co-reporter. "Now, when you say 'it's a nonissue,'" said Todd, "you're talking about race relations or the survey?"

I was really impressed. Todd didn't raise his voice, but he was firm. It was like he'd heard the implied *Drop it* in Mr. Michaels's tone and said, *No.*

Mr. Michaels sighed. "Race relations in Hillsdale are excellent," he said. "Both in Hillsdale the town and Hillsdale the school. And I don't want the school paper stirring up a lot of trouble just because you want to get a 'scoop.'"

"So you think whites and blacks at Hillsdale get along perfectly?" said Todd.

"I wouldn't say *perfectly*," said Mr. Michaels. "Nothing's perfect." He smirked, like he'd just come up with this little bon mot all on his own. "But the students of Hillsdale do live in harmony with one another."

There was silence. Todd was bent over his note-book, scribbling Mr. Michaels's words. Mr. Michaels toyed with the "# 1 PRINCIPAL" paperweight on his desk. I took a deep breath, remembering how much work Todd had already done to make this interview happen. Was I really going to sit there like some kind of deaf-mute?

"May I ask on what you're basing the idea that Hillsdale students live in racial harmony ?"

Mr. Michaels turned in my direction. "I'm sorry?" he said.

It was scary to have an authority figure looking at me with such obvious dislike. I *hate* when people, espe-cially grown-ups, are mad at or disappointed in me. But now Todd was looking up at me, too, and it was like he was saying, *You can do it. You can do it.* I forced myself to meet Mr. Michaels's gaze. "Well, have you discussed the issue with members of the student body, or . . ." I couldn't think of another way he would know, so I just said, "or is it just your sense of things?"

He laughed, but it was clear he didn't think what I'd said was funny. "Well, I hardly see race riots as I walk through the building. This isn't Watts." He paused and looked at us. "Watts was—"

"A housing project in L.A. that exploded in racial

violence in 1965," said Todd. "We know. And is that your definition of racial tension—Watts?"

I couldn't *believe* how cool this was. How did Todd know about *Watts?*

"Now, Mr. Kincaid, let's not get carried away. I'm not saying the school would have to *explode* for us to look at the issue."

"Well, what *would* it take?" My question startled me almost as much as it seemed to startle Mr. Michaels.

"What would *what* take, Miss Lewis?" If Mr. Michaels had been trying to conceal his annoyance before, now it was pretty evident that he didn't care to bother. He'd snapped his question at me like a rubber band.

I tried to keep my voice from shaking as I repeated my question. "What would it take for you to look at racial issues at Hillsdale?"

"A great deal more than two students claiming there is a problem."

"Can you be more specific?" asked Todd.

Just then the intercom on Mr. Michaels's phone beeped. He picked up the receiver, holding up his hand to quiet us even though we weren't talking. "Yes?" He listened to a voice on the other end. "Fine."

He hung up the phone and stood up. "I'm sorry, kids, but we'll have to cut this interview short. I'm needed immediately in Mr. Rubin's office." Mr. Rubin is the vice principal.

"Sure," said Todd. "We understand. Maybe we'll be able to follow up on some of these questions another time."

"Maybe," said Mr. Michaels, but he said it like, *In your dreams, baby.*

"We appreciate your time," I said. I liked the way it sounded—professional.

We both shook Mr. Michaels's hand and then we left. Standing in the corridor right outside his office, Todd slapped me five. "Well done, Reporter Lewis."

"Are you kidding?! *You're* the one who was amazing," I said, squeezing his arm. "How did you know about Watts?"

Todd looked at me like I was the whitest person he'd ever laid eyes on. "It's kind of important," he said.

"Right," I said. "Of course."

We stood in the hallway for a few more minutes, going over the interview and debating whether we had enough material for an article. Neither of us thought we did, so we figured the only thing to do was interview Dr. Thomas, Superintendent of Schools. The idea of interviewing Dr. Thomas completely freaked me out, but Todd assured me it would be fine and said he'd call to set up the interview. When the bell rang, Todd had to run to class. He was already halfway down the hall when I realized something. I called his name and ran to catch up with him.

"Hey," I said, panting slightly from my brief dash down the corridor. Dr. Emerson was right—it *was* time for an exercise regime. "I just realized something."

"What?" asked Todd.

I looked around to make sure no one was listening to us, feeling a little melodramatic but also truly afraid of being overheard. "He never came out of his office."

"What do you mean?"

"Mr. Michaels," I said, lowering my voice to a whisper. "He said he had to go to a meeting in Mr. Rubin's office immediately. But he never left his."

THIRTEEN
. . .

THE FIFTH AND SIXTH COMMANDMENTS:
THOU SHALT DISPOSE OF THINE EX'S
PARAPHERNALIA (AND WHILE YOU'RE AT IT,
GET OFF YOUR BUTT AND EXERCISE!)

THE TWENTY MINUTES TODD and I spent in Mr. Michaels's office and the ten we spent talking about the interview afterward represented the only half hour since I'd seen Max at the movies with Anya that I hadn't spent thinking about him. I wished Dr. Emerson had been a little more specific about the time it was going to take to get from heartbreak to happiness. I also wished I hadn't already broken the second and fourth commandments, since that was undoubtedly delaying my arrival.

Friday afternoon Martha had to meet with her SAT tutor and Clara had a doctor's appointment. Being alone made me profoundly depressed, but taking the pint of gelato out of the freezer didn't. It made me feel better. Much better. One spoonful. Two spoonfuls. Things were definitely looking up.

Unfortunately, halfway through the container, I remembered Dr. Emerson. In her chapter The Most Beautiful Girl in the World Is _____ [insert your name here], she specifically says, Now is not the time to drown your sorrows in high-calorie snacks! This significantly decreased the pleasure I'd been taking in every creamy mouthful. But it wasn't like I was eating *ice cream*. Now *there's* a high-calorie snack. Gelato's practically *health food*. It's *European*, for heaven's sake.

I should have left it at that, but being me, I had to ruin everything by trying to confirm my "Gelato's the new baby carrots" theory with hard facts. And according to the side of the container, with my final swallow I'd just finished consuming over twelve hundred calories— or roughly 280 pounds—of baby carrots.

This was definitely not good. But it wasn't like I was about to go puke up a pint of gelato. WWDED (What Would Dr. Emerson Do)?

Go forth and fulfill my commandments.

I headed upstairs to my room, where I started rummaging through my CD collection. It wasn't exactly ard to find the ones from Max—they stood out like a goth at Carnegie Hall. Artists whose CDs Jennifer purchased for herself: ABBA, David Bowie, Liz Phair, The Dixie Chicks. Artists whose CDs Max burned for Jennifer: The Killers, Wilco, The Arcade Fire, Clap Your Hands Say Yeah. Seeing his handwriting on the CDs made me start to get all depressed again, so I dumped the collection in a shoe box as fast as I could. Then I shoved the box all the way to the back of my closet, along with a Harvard T-shirt I'd borrowed from him and never returned, and the profile he'd made me for my birthday.

I was expecting Clara at seven. Todd and Martha had invited us to go bowling with them (like they couldn't have done that on their *first* date, not that I'm bitter or anything), but since leaving the house required way more get-up-and-go than I had in my arsenal, Clara and I would be staying in for the evening (as my oldest friend in the world, Clara was loyally under house arrest as long as I needed her to be).

There was still an hour before Clara would be over, so I called my dad, who wanted to drive up to Westchester and take me to dinner immediately and/or any night I was free (like there was a night I *wasn't*). But even if I could have imagined a future when all my free time wouldn't be spent within the confines of my own house (preferably in my own bed), no way did that future include braving the dining establishments of West-chester County. When the time was right, I assured him, I'd make my way to the city. In the background, Jay shouted for me to pick a date and e-mail him my dream menu so he could prepare it.

The conversation ending when it did gave me just enough time to tackle commandment number six. I got out my mom's yoga mat and her *Hot Yoga* DVD. As far as I could tell, yoga was actually killing two command-ments with one stone since it was A) exercise and B) *definitely* a hobby I could not have pursued while I was going out with Max, considering every time he saw a sign announcing a meeting of the Hillsdale High Yoga Association (HiYA), he practically passed out from laughing so hard.

Danny came into the den just as I was trying to get into downward-facing dog, a position that is clearly incompatible with having eaten a pint of gelato.

"Yo, what up?" he asked. Then he answered his own question, "Your *ass*!" and started cracking up.

"You're hilarious, Danny," I said. My voice was less authoritative than I would have liked it to be, what with my being upside-down and about to hurl.

Danny plopped down on the sofa. "You know, you shouldn't get hung up on one guy like this," he said, stretching. "You should be like me. Play the field." As if on cue, his cell phone began to play its new ring, "Big Pimpin'." Danny checked to see who was calling, then put the still-ringing phone back in his pocket. "'Cause the babe beautiful enough to pin the D-man down ain't been born yet."

"That's really touching, Daniel," I said, dropping into cobra. "I think I might start crying."

"All I'm saying is, you gotta get over this guy, dig?"

Could he not see that was exactly what I was *trying* to do? I know yoga's supposed to be calming, but somehow it wasn't having that effect on me. Or maybe *Danny* wasn't having that effect on me. I rolled over onto my back and glared at him. "Don't make me kill you, D-Man."

Danny made a big show of feigning terror, creeping out of the room as if I had a bead on him with an automatic weapon. "Easy there, woman," he said. And then he was gone.

I looked at the clock. Six forty-five. Clara was coming over at seven. Only fifteen more minutes of yoga.

Did something you did once and never attempted again qualify as an exercise *routine*?

"Jenny, honey," called my mom, "can I get your opinion on something?"

Normally it's really annoying when I'm doing something and my mother interrupts, but normally the thing

I'm doing when she interrupts me isn't yoga. I took the stairs two at a time.

"What's up?" I asked. The room wasn't exactly *strewn* with clothes, but there was definitely more than the usual amount of disorder in evidence. She was holding two different earrings up to her face and studying herself in the mirror over her dresser.

"Which earrings do you prefer?" I walked over to her. She was wearing a dark blue sweater that made her hair look really blond, and a white, wool miniskirt. The whole thing was a little too sexy for a mom, if you want my opinion.

Despite her having managed to put together a fairly decent (or indecent, depending on your perspective) outfit, the earrings she was holding up were awful. One was this long, dangly silver-turquoise thing that looked like she'd bought it off a Grateful Dead fan circa 1970; the other was a really tacky piece of costume jewelry that could only have been a present from Nana. I shook my head to indicate what a disaster they were.

"Both?" she asked, turning from the mirror to face me.

I closed my eyes and held up my hand as if to ward off the sight before me. "The horror," I said. Then I opened her jewelry box and dug through it until I found the pair of pearls I was looking for.

"Aren't those a little conservative?" she asked, seeing what I'd chosen

I looked her up and down. "Let me tell you, a little conservative's not always a bad thing," I said. "And where are you going tonight, anyway? Isn't it book club night?"

"Um, yeah," she said. But she said it the way I used to say, "Um, yeah," when Max and I were going over to his house and she'd ask if his parents were going to be there.

"*And* . . . ?" I said.

"*And* . . . ?" she repeated, reaching for the pearls in my hand. At the last second, I closed my fingers around them and pulled my hand to my chest.

Sometimes I think I will make an *excellent* mom.

"*And* . . . ?" I repeated.

My mom sighed like *I* was the one who was being immature. "*And* we might get a drink after," she said.

"Oh," I said. Suddenly I wasn't in the mood to know just who "we" were. I put the earrings on her dresser without saying anything.

Was my mother going on a *date? Now? Now*, when my heart had just been stomped on? Couldn't she wait until a year from now? Or, better yet, *two* years from now, when I'd be off at college and wouldn't have to see her getting all dressed up for a night on the town while

I schlepped around the house in sweatpants and my dad's ancient Wesleyan sweatshirt?

"Honey, are you okay?" My mom's voice was full of concern, but I wasn't buying it for a minute. If she cared one *iota* for my well-being, she would never have chosen this as the moment to revisit her All Men Suck philosophy.

Luckily, right then I heard the beep of the alarm code being punched in, which meant Clara had arrived. I backed out of the room like my mom was a potentially dangerous animal I couldn't take my eyes off for a second.

As I went downstairs to meet Clara, I tried to feel as excited as I used to feel about a Friday night with Max. Like Dr. Emerson says, Friends are as precious as boyfriends. Don't think of this time with your friends as somehow second-rate just because you're not in a relationship.

To show just how not second-rate I thought being with Clara was, I walked into the kitchen with a gigantic smile on my face, ready to embark upon a Friday night in the company of my dearest friend with my best foot forward.

Clara dropped her bag on a chair, took one look at me, and scowled. "What's with you?" she asked.

I let my face fall. "I don't want to be one of those girls who isn't happy unless she has a boyfriend. Dr.

Emerson says it's bad to think of your friends as fall-back."

"That's so funny," she said, taking off her coat. "Because I think it's bad to think of Dr. Emerson *at all.*"

I ignored her. "I'm up to commandment number eight," I said. I took her coat and hung it on the coatrack. "I'm supposed to take a vacation."

"Want to come to Florida with me for spring break?" she asked, perching on the kitchen counter. Clara's grandmother had recently been moved to an assisted living facility, and her family was going to check on how she was doing.

I shook my head and got down two glasses from the cabinet. "Dr. Emerson says it's only a few short steps from heartache to happiness," I said, pouring us each some seltzer.

"Maybe you and Dr. Feelgood have different definitions of short," said Clara. She took a glass from me.

"Maybe," I said. "Or maybe we have different definitions of *happiness.*" I was thinking of the women in my mom's book group. Was *that* the "happiness" I was working toward?

"Then to hell with her," said Clara. She lifted her glass. "A toast," she said. "To happiness à la Jennifer."

"If there *is* such a thing," I said, unable to remember a time when I didn't feel sad every minute of every day.

171

But when I touched my glass to hers and drank, I felt better, if only infinitesimally so. Because when you don't know how long it will take you to get from heartache to happiness or even what happiness will look like once you get there, it's important to have your best friend along for the trip.

I grabbed a box of chocolate-chip cookies from the pantry, and we headed to the den to watch anything other than *All the President's Men*.

FOURTEEN

. . .

THE EIGHTH COMMANDMENT: THOU SHALT CHANGE THY SCENERY

I REALIZE GOING TO DINNER in Manhattan isn't exactly a Caribbean vacation, but when you're a junior in high school, it's not like you can slap down your AmEx Gold Card and trade in a few sick days for a week of sun and fun. In lieu of a tropical cruise, I took advantage of Jay's offer to cook me my dream meal, inviting myself to their place for dinner the first Friday of spring break. After all, if you live in the 'burbs, then 212, while it may not be a vacation, is definitely a change of scenery.

Over my favorite dinner (seared tuna, asparagus, and mashed potatoes), I told them all about Dr. Emerson and how I wasn't sure I was doing the program right since, despite having more or less fulfilled the first eight commandments, I still felt so bad all the time.

"Well, it can take a long time to get over a breakup," said my dad.

"God," said Jay, "when I was just out of college, I had the *worst* breakup. I'd barely recovered by my thirtieth birthday."

"Thanks, Jay," I said. "That's just what I wanted to hear."

"Forget I said anything," he said, miming drawing a zipper across his lips. "Here——" He poured some wine into my glass and put some more of the perfectly cooked fish he'd made on my plate. "Eat. Drink. Be merry."

"When your mom and I split up, I felt like a ghost," said my dad, swirling the last of his wine around in his glass. He shook his head at the memory. "God, that was a lousy time."

I nearly choked on my new potatoes. "*What?* But you were the dump*er*, not the dump*ee*."

My dad laughed. "Honey, it's not black and white like that. I mean, obviously in our case there were reasons external for the demise of the marriage"——he gestured in a way that I guess was meant to indicate the apartment, Jay, and my dad's sexual orientation in general——"but I think it's just sad when a relationship ends. Even if one is the 'dumper.'" He put air quotes around dumper.

"Oh," I said. Then I thought about it. "Well, I highly doubt Max is sad, what with his *having a new girlfriend already*." I'd already told my dad about Max and Anya, but apparently he needed a refresher course.

Jay went over to the special refrigerator where they keep their wine and hunted around for a minute before slipping a bottle out from the middle rack and then opening it with this fancy opener they have. I tried not to think about Max and the wine cellar.

"You shouldn't compare people's outsides with your insides," said Jay. He uncovered the platter of cheeses on the counter. Then he came back to the table carrying the wine. "And anyway, *you* could have a new *boyfriend* if you want one."

"God, you sound like Dr. Emerson," I said. Had these people not *gone* to high school? Even if ninety percent of the student body weren't off-limits because they're either A) gross, B) taken, or C) out of my league (i.e., President of the Student Council, soccer star, Most Popular, Best Looking, need I say more?), how, exactly, was I supposed to manufacture a romance with an arbitrarily chosen classmate? Was I just supposed to grab a seat next to some guy in math one day and give him a soul kiss?

Sure. Right after I skipped naked through the cafeteria singing "The Star-Spangled Banner" at the top of my lungs.

"Yes, but unlike Dr. Emerson, *I* am willing to *provide* you with your new boyfriend," said Jay, refilling my dad's glass and his own.

"Oh, God, don't start in with Elmo," I said.

"Eugene!" said Jay. He sat down. "And I'm telling you, he's a fox. I'll show you a picture after dinner."

Unfortunately the "picture" Jay showed me—from a Fourth of July party they'd thrown in the Hamptons last summer—was of the back of Eugene's head. Jay kept insisting you can tell a lot from the back of a person's head (like how he's got all his hair), but I pointed out that at seventeen I was less worried about premature balding than guys in their forties probably were.

It took me forever to fall asleep, and it wasn't because I was overwhelmed by the incredible sex appeal of the back of Eugene's full head of hair. I kept thinking about what Jay and my dad had said about Max, about how he was probably sad about our breakup. Did he *miss* me? Was he sad that we weren't together anymore?

Because the thing was, I missed him. Even though I'd never admit it to anyone, even though I was really, really, *really* trying to go from heartache to happiness, all I hoped every morning when I arrived at school was that Max would be waiting at my locker, ready to fall to his knees and beg me to take him back. And I didn't want that to happen so I could tell him to go to hell. I didn't want it to happen so I could tell him I wouldn't take him back if he were the last man on Earth.

I wanted it to happen so he would be my boyfriend again.

FIFTEEN

. . .

NOBODY DOES IT BETTER—THAN YOU!

THE DAY BEFORE our interview with Superintendent Thomas, Mr. Barton asked me and Todd to stay after the *Spectator* meeting for a few minutes.

"So, you two ready?" he asked, sitting with his feet up on the conference table.

"Ready as we'll ever be," said Todd.

"Definitely," I said, hoping my voice didn't convey my inability to focus on anything other than the fact that Max and Anya had once again scuttled out of the office—holding hands—the second the meeting ended.

Mr. Barton nodded. "Got your interview questions?"

Todd took out the list of questions we'd agreed on. Mr. Barton looked them over, then handed them back to Todd. "These look good," he said. "Just remember, you'll—"

"—find additional questions in your answers," Todd and I said in unison. Mr. Barton's always saying that's the cardinal rule of interviewing.

He smiled, clearly pleased at how thoroughly we'd learned his lesson. "I have the utmost confidence in the two of you," he said. "You're ready for prime time."

"Thanks," we said together.

Mr. Barton scratched thoughtfully at his beard, then dropped his feet to the ground. "Even though you don't need it, let me give you one more piece of advice," he said.

"Which is?" I figured he was going to say that we should try to trip Dr. Thomas up with Mr. Michaels's answers or that it's important to take extremely careful notes during an interview. So what he actually said came as a complete and total surprise.

"Follow the money." He took a minute to let his words sink in, then stood up. "Class dismissed."

♥ ♥ ♥

Todd drove us to the interview Tuesday after school, and even though the district's central office isn't far from the high school, it felt like we'd entered a different universe. Located in a low-slung, stucco building, it looked more like a strip mall than a school, and inside there was a lot of beige carpeting and windows that didn't open and people hurrying around carrying stacks of xeroxed packets.

Right away, Dr. Thomas seemed a lot smoother than Mr. Michaels. He invited us to have a seat on a sofa by the window, and he sat in a chair facing us, like we were just three people getting together for a social visit instead of a couple of kids trying to interview the super-intendent of schools.

"We appreciate your taking the time to talk to us," said Todd, after Dr. Thomas had asked if we wanted any-thing to drink. I was actually a little thirsty, but I said no, since I felt weird asking if I could have a glass of water. Todd said no, too.

"Of course. I'm glad to see students taking initiative like this," said Dr. Thomas. He looked younger than Mr. Michaels, but I wondered if it was just that he had a full head of hair. Thinking of that made me think of my dad and Jay, which made me think of Eugene, which made me think of Max.

Was there ever going to be a second in my life when every single thing I saw didn't remind me of Max?

"We'd like to start by getting your impression of race relations in the Hillsdale school district," said Todd.

"Well, first off, let me start by saying how very

proud I am of what a diverse population Hillsdale has," said Dr. Thomas. "Students in the Hillsdale district have the opportunity to study with students of different ethnicities, different racial backgrounds, different religions. That's one of the most extraordinary things about the district."

"We were interested in doing a survey about that diversity," I said, "but Mr. Michaels said no."

Dr. Thomas nodded, like we'd just confirmed his point instead of contradicting it. "Well, if Mr. Michaels says a questionnaire of the sort that you're describing isn't a good idea for the school, I'm sure he's right."

"We think there *are* racial issues at Hillsdale," said Todd. "Segregation, for example. And we'd like to investigate them."

"You talk to me about segregation," said Dr. Thomas, smiling, "and yet I'm sitting here looking at a fairly diverse pair of reporters." His glance took in me, the white girl, and Todd, the black boy; then he sat back in his chair like we'd proved his point way better than he ever could have.

"It's not that we're saying black people and white people at Hillsdale *hate* each other," I said. "But there are a lot of classes that are all white students and a lot of classes that are all black students. And there's no forum for discussing race, like there is for talking about gender and sex and . . . stuff." I couldn't believe I'd just said sex to the superintendent of schools. My face flushed, and I really wished I'd asked for that glass of water.

"Well, I'm sure if there were a need for such a forum, there would be one," Dr. Thomas said. He crossed his ankle over his knee.

"How can we prove there's a need for one if we can't ask students the questions that would *show* there's a need for one?" Todd's voice stayed even, but I could tell he was getting frustrated with Dr. Thomas's slick answers.

"Listen," said Dr. Thomas, looking directly at Todd, "race is a sensitive issue. I don't have to tell you that." Was he talking just to Todd or to both of us? "And while I'm sure your motives are admirable, they could easily be misinterpreted."

"In other words, don't stir up trouble," said Todd.

"I wouldn't put it in those terms, exactly," said Dr. Thomas. "I would say it's more that as a student you have a different perspective on the situation than someone like Mr. Michaels, someone who can be objective." He still seemed to be speaking only to Todd.

"Are you saying that because I'm black?" asked Todd.

"I'm saying that because you're a student," said Dr. Thomas evenly. "And I resent the implication in your question."

Todd stood up. I didn't know what to do. Was the interview over? Tucking his notebook back into his bag, Todd looked at Dr. Thomas. "I did a little casual research," he said. "There are one hundred and twenty students in this year's graduating class. Eighteen of them are black. Ten of them are Latino. And in three of my four AP classes, I'm the only black student."

Dr. Thomas didn't blink. "Race is not a factor in determining who does and who does not get into AP classes."

"Of course it isn't," said Todd. "Of course it isn't." And then he nodded at Dr. Thomas and walked out of the office.

"Um, thanks for your time," I said, scurrying to catch up with Todd. "Really."

When I got to the parking lot, Todd was leaning against his car, arms folded across his chest.

"Hi," I said. I really had no idea what to say about what had just happened.

"What do you think Mr. Barton meant when he said, follow the money."

"It's from *All the President's Men*," I said, glad that for once I was the one who could explain a reference to Todd. "Woodward and Bernstein are trying to figure out who broke into the Watergate and spied on the Democratic National Committee, and when it starts to look like it was people with ties to the Republicans, Deep Throat tells them to follow the money."

"Meaning?"

"Meaning . . . find out who has the most to lose in a given situation. Who's invested in a certain outcome. Those are the people who are going to be willing to make sure the outcome they want is the outcome they get."

"Well, Dr. Thomas probably takes home a nice six-figure salary," said Todd. "He's certainly going to be invested in everything looking hunky-dory at Hillsdale." He laughed briefly. "And by 'hunky', I mean 'honkey.'"

Suddenly I started laughing. I couldn't help it—the combination of how tense I'd been sitting in Dr. Thomas's office and Todd's joke. I just lost it. A second later, Todd did, too, and it took us a long while to get ourselves under control.

♥ ♥ ♥

When I got home, I was still thinking about what had happened with Dr. Thomas. Because of the article, I was seeing a whole other side of Hillsdale, and I had the feeling most kids at Hillsdale were the way I'd been before—only seeing one little part of the school and thinking it was the whole institution. I remembered eighth grade, when one of the boys in my class complained that he had to sit through the lesson on menstruation in health class, and the teacher said boys have to learn about girls' bodies and girls have to learn about boys'. So why couldn't we do the same thing with black students and white students? Why was it important for a thirteen-year-old boy to know what a tampon is, but not for Danny to know if he's insulting the black kids in his classes every time he refers to one of his friends as his "homey"?

I would probably have kept thinking about the interview all afternoon if I hadn't checked my e-mail. As it was, though, the minute I opened the only letter in my inbox and its attachment, all thoughts of what had happened in Dr. Thomas's office evaporated. When I dialed Clara's and Martha's cell phones and told them to get over to my house immediately, it definitely wasn't because I wanted their insights into the current state of race relations at Hillsdale.

SIXTEEN

• • •

WHO SAYS YES TO LIFE? YOU DO!

"WELL, HE'S DEFINITELY CUTE," said Martha. Which was true. Eugene's brown hair was peppered with blond streaks that looked summertime natural. He had a great smile, and there was no denying that his shoulders filled out the T-shirt he was wearing quite nicely. Since he was sitting down on the steps of the back deck at my dad and Jay's Hamptons house, it was hard to know how tall he was, but his legs did reach from the third step of the deck to the ground, and his torso looked to be normal length. So if you added up an average-size top half and an at-least-longish bottom half, you couldn't exactly get a dwarf.

All Jay's e-mail said was, *The front's even better than the back.* I'd had no idea what he was talking about. Even after I'd opened the attachment it took me a minute to realize who the picture he'd sent me was *of*.

186

"So, I mean, what happens now?" Clara asked, leaning over my shoulder and staring at the screen.

I shrugged. "Jay didn't even say if he, like, gave him my number or anything," I said.

Martha screamed. "You mean he could just call here? Like, right now?"

As if it had just rung, we all stared at the phone.

Clara was the first to speak. "But what would you *talk* to him about? I mean, if he does call?"

"*I* don't know," I said, suddenly annoyed. What, did Clara think I'd taken some special secret dating class while she and Martha were stuck in sophomore English?

Martha went over and sat on my beanbag chair. "I'm sure you'll find things to talk about," she said.

I wanted to share Martha's confidence, but unfortunately, I couldn't. "Like what?" I asked.

"Like . . ." She thought for a minute. "Well, like how many brothers and sisters you have."

"I have one brother. He's thirteen, and he thinks he's Barry White." I looked at my watch. "Hey, that's a whole ten seconds of conversation. Better be careful or I'll go over my minutes this month."

"Don't be negative," said Martha. "Besides, when's the last time you were at a loss for words?"

"Um, *hello*! When's the last time I was on a blind date?"

187

"I don't think it's technically a blind date if you've seen the person," said Clara. She flopped back on my bed and started tossing a pillow at the ceiling and letting it fall on her face.

"What if he's a total loser?" I asked.

"No way," said Martha. "*Look* at him. Does he *look* like a total loser?" She was right. With his chiseled jaw and that wide, easy smile, Eugene (despite his name) looked like the exact opposite of a loser.

He looked like a stud.

"Why does he need to be fixed up on a blind date if he's not a loser," I pointed out. "Why doesn't he have a girlfriend?"

"Why do *you* need to be fixed up on a blind date? *You're* not a loser," said Martha.

"Yeah," said Clara. "You just happened to have gotten dumped by one."

"Is this conversation supposed to be making me feel better?" I asked.

"Okay," said Martha, "here's the deal." She closed her eyes and thought about it for a second, then opened them, leaned forward, and started talking. "He and his family have lived in London for the past ten years. He had a girlfriend there, they were madly in love. Then, in September, the family moves to New York. Over Christmas, when he goes back to London, the girl says she can't deal with the long-distance thing and she dumps him. He's heartbroken, but now he finally feels ready to love again. Only, since he goes to an all-boys school, he doesn't know any American girls."

I was too amazed by Martha's having made up such a complicated story extemporaneously to quibble over its plausibility. "You should be a novelist," I said. "Seriously."

Martha leaned back. "Do you think he has a British accent?" she asked dreamily.

I knew I was supposed to be thinking about Eugene for Eugene's sake, but I couldn't help imagining how Max would feel if he saw me leaving school in the company of my cute new British boyfriend with the broad shoulders and sun-kissed hair. Probably Eugene knew about all kinds of cool British bands that hadn't yet made it across the Atlantic. He and Max would meet at some Hillsdale party, and Eugene would be like, *Wow, man, your taste in bands is so five minutes ago*. That would kill Max.

Jay called right before dinner to ask if I'd gotten the picture, but as soon as I started lobbing questions at him, he just said, *All in good time*, which if you ask me is even more annoying than *Only the Shadow knows*.

Long after Clara and Martha left, I kept thinking about Eugene. I pictured us running into Max and Anya at a fancy Manhattan restaurant, where they'd just been told there weren't any tables, but the maitre d', knowing Eugene by name, would sweep us off to the best table in the house. Eugene probably drove one of those cute little British sports cars, which he'd lend me (after teaching me how to drive a stick shift, natch). I pictured Max watching me pull out of the student parking lot, cool underground music blasting, top down, tires screeching as I peeled onto Mountain View Road. Once I had a new boyfriend, Max and I could be friends again, and I'd do stuff like burn him copies of Eugene's music. *Here you go*, I'd say, tossing a CD in his direction after a *Spectator* meeting. *Eugene just got this from a friend of his who's an independent music producer. These guys are the hottest thing in London.*

The problem was, all of my fantasies of me and Eugene ended with the same by now all-too-familiar ending: Max falling to his knees outside my locker and begging me to take him back. Then I'd apologize profusely to Eugene, return the keys to the MG, and go off with Max, while Anya tried (unsuccessfully) to get her hair out of her tearstained face.

I knew I wasn't approaching the whole "plenty of fish in the sea" thing quite right, but there didn't seem to be anything I could do about it.

♥ ♥ ♥

Todd and I were working on our article twenty-four/
seven, even delegating most of our other *Spectator* duties
to the contributing editors (not, needless to say, Anya),
but no matter how much time we put in, it never
seemed to get any better. Every time Mr. Barton read a
draft, he said the same thing, "What's the story?" And
even though we were getting pretty irritated with him,
neither of us could answer Mr. Barton's question. We
had some cool quotes. We had some interesting theo-
ries. But there was no smoking gun.

"We can't run this," said Todd on Wednesday afternoon. The paper was going to the printer a week from
Friday, which meant production would start on Monday.
Which meant that, given what we had, our article
wasn't going to be running in the May issue. Which
meant it wouldn't be running at *all*, since there's not
really a June issue of the *Spectator*, just a special graduation issue that comes out the last day of school and is
comprised exclusively of the seniors' last will and testaments.

"This sucks," I said. "I can't believe we did all this
work for nothing."

Todd shook his head. It was hard to know which of
us was more upset.

"Look," I said, "we can't despair. We'll find our
smoking gun. *Something* has to happen."

He shrugged. "What, like an anonymous phone call?"

"Hey, anything's possible."

♥ ♥ ♥

The weird thing was, as I was walking out to the parking lot, I *did* get an anonymous phone call. Or at least a phone call from a number I didn't recognize. For an insane second, I thought that maybe it was Dr. Thomas or Mr. Michaels calling to arrange a secret meeting at which he would expose a horrifying malfeasance the other man had committed. It took about two rings for me to figure out that, in addition to all the other reasons such a scenario was highly unlikely, neither of them had my cell number.

"Hello?"

"Hi, is this Jennifer?" The voice on the other end of the line didn't exactly clear up the confusion about who was calling, since I'd definitely never heard it before.

"This is Jennifer." Our conversation had a touch of *Scream* to it. I glanced around the parking lot, glad to see more than a few of my fellow students heading to their cars.

"This is Gene Barry."

Apparently this was supposed to mean something to me.

"Uh, hi, Gene Barry," I said. I wondered if it was a telemarketer.

There was a pause.

"You have no idea who I am, do you?" He laughed and said, "Okay, this phone call has suddenly gotten a lot more embarrassing. Ah, I got your number from Jay Friedman. He said—"

I don't know what you're supposed to do when a person calls you for a blind date, but I'm pretty sure what I did isn't it. Because what *I* did was trip over a crack in the asphalt and send my cell flying across the parking lot and under a Chevy Blazer the size of California.

Needless to say, by the time I'd crawled under the truck and recovered my phone, the call had been disconnected. At least my cell was still working, which was a minor miracle. But now I had no idea what I was supposed to do. Should I call him back? Or was I supposed to let *him* call *me* back? I've read enough *Seventeen* articles to know it's good to play hard to get, but maybe hurling the phone to the ground when a guy says who's calling *and* not calling him back was overkill.

The question proved to be moot when my phone rang a minute later with the same no-longer-unfamiliar number.

"Hi," I said.

"Okay, I'm sensing you'd rather we not meet," said Eugene. Or Gene, as he was apparently called.

"No, no," I said quickly. I liked his voice. Even though there was no trace of a British accent, it was deep and surprisingly calm. If I had to call a total stranger twice in two minutes, my voice would be so high-pitched only a dog could hear it. "I'm glad you called. I just didn't—" There were so many things I "didn't" that I wasn't sure where to start. "I didn't know you're called Gene. Jay called you Eugene."

"Yeah, Jay and my grandmother are the only people who still call me that," he said.

"Oh." Okay, this was officially incredibly weird. I remembered my conversation with Martha and Clara, but now didn't seem like a good time to ask Gene if he had any brothers or sisters. "I'm not usually this inarticulate," is what I finally settled on. "You caught me off guard."

"You mean Jay hasn't been calling you twice a day, every day, and talking me up?"

I wanted to die. "Tell me he hasn't been doing that."

"I hate to lie to you before we've even met."

"I feel like such a dork."

"*You* feel like a dork? Hey, *I'm* the one who's been looking at pictures of *you* for the past week."

"Pictures? Plural?" I wanted to *kill* Jay. I wanted to

kill myself. I wanted to kill Gene. I wanted to kill every-one who knew about this whole situation. I made a hit list in my head to distract me from my complete humil-iation.

"One a day for the past week. But I think he's running low. The last one looks like it might be circa graduation from kindergarten."

"I'm surprised you didn't hold out for the one where I'm crawling around naked on the bearskin rug."

Gene laughed. "I should have."

There was a pause. "He sent me a picture of you, too," I said quickly into the silence.

"No wonder you hung up on me," he said, laughing again.

"Oh, no," I said. "It was . . . fine. I mean, good. It was a good picture of you. Or, I mean, I don't know what you really look like, so I just mean it . . . I didn't mean to hang up on you before. I tripped." *And to tell the truth, right about now I wouldn't mind tripping again.*

I don't know if Gene was as embarrassed as I was or if he had the feeling our conversation had peaked some-where around the bearskin rug. Either way, he said, "Clearly Jay's not going to leave us alone until we meet each other."

"Clearly," I said.

"So, I propose we meet."

"Okay," I said. Then I wasn't sure what to say next.

"Um, would you like me to come up to Westchester? Jay said you live in—"

"No!" I said quickly. It was one thing for Max to see me and my British boyfriend flying along Mountain View Road in a convertible MG, laughing and making out en route to a weekend at Mohonk. It was quite another for him to see me and a guy my dad's boyfriend practically forced to take me out on a blind date eating our General Tso's Chicken in awkward silence, having run out of things to talk about over the hot and sour soup.

My abrupt response seemed to have startled Gene into silence, so I quickly added, "I mean, it's way more fun to do something in the city."

"Sure," he said. "I could plan some incredibly urbane outing."

As soon as Gene said urbane, I realized I hadn't used a single SAT word in our entire conversation. Sadly, I decided to rectify that by saying, "Scintillating." *Scintillating?*

"The thing is," he said, ignoring my malapropism, "it's my grandmother's seventy-fifth birthday Friday, so I'm kind of under house arrest until Saturday night. Do you want to do something then?"

Even though it should have been clear to me for at

least a minute or two that this conversation was going to end in our making a date, the idea that I would actually be meeting Gene face-to-face didn't become concrete until he mentioned Saturday night. Saturday night was real. Saturday night would come (and sooner, rather than later).

Needless to say, I didn't offer up this *scintillating* insight. Instead I took refuge in the banal. "Great."

"Why don't I e-mail you before then with a plan?"

"You have my e-mail address?"

"I'm pretty sure I have your Social Security number. Jay's very thorough."

"Apparently." Another pause. "Well, thanks for calling," I said. "And say happy birthday to your grandma for me." *Had I just said that? What was my problem? Hi, Grandma, Happy Birthday. That's from this random girl Jennifer you've never met. Oh, wait, I've never met her either.*

Gene was either too polite or too desperate to get off the phone to point out how retarded my birthday greeting to his grandmother was. "I will," he said. "And, I guess I'll see you Saturday."

"Yeah," I said. "Bye."

"Bye."

I flipped my phone shut. So that was Gene. He didn't sound dorky. He sounded nice. He sounded funny. Maybe we'd go on our date and fall madly in love and by next week I'd be like, "Max who?"

And then with my luck, a few months from now Eugene and I would be sitting in front of my house in his MG with the top down, some bootlegged concert blasting from the stereo, and he'd turn to me and go, "You know, I've been thinking about this a lot lately, and I want us to just be friends."

Even though we'd never met, imagining being dumped by Gene made me want to die. What was the *point* of going out with someone? What was the *point* of falling in love? The whole thing was enough to make me wish I'd been born in one of those countries where they still have arranged marriages. I mean, okay, yes, it would certainly suck not being allowed to drive or vote and having to ask a man's permission to leave the house.

But at least you wouldn't have to worry about getting dumped.

SEVENTEEN

. . .

I BELIEVE IN ME!

GENE'S E-MAIL CAME the next night while I was sitting at my desk working on a *Hamlet* essay. "Discuss Hamlet's treatment of Ophelia and what it indicates about his character." I'd only chosen to answer this question because Hamlet goes out with Ophelia and then basically dumps her for no reason, and I'd thought writing about what a total unfeeling jerk Hamlet is would be really satisfying. Unfortunately, I'd underestimated just how big a role the word "jerk" played in my thesis. Once I realized this, why the paper wasn't exactly writing itself became less of a mystery.

hey,

read Gene's e-mail,

i have an idea for saturday night. kind of random but hopefully cool. let's meet at 140 ludlow street at 8.

do you know that neighborhood? if not, i could pick you up at your dad and jay's place. g.

Ludlow Street was the Lower East Side, and I only kind of knew my way around there.

But how lame would it be to need an escort from my dad's apartment to Ludlow Street? I might as well pin a little tag to my shirt, PLEASE LOOK AFTER THIS BEAR. THANK YOU.

I wrote:

sounds good. see you at 8. j

Then I hit SEND, which I regretted more or less immediately. I should have written something clever and witty involving the words "random but cool." I could have used a well-chosen quote from *Hamlet*. "To be random but cool or not to be random but cool, that is the question."

Just thinking of having written something like that made me embarrassed for myself. I picked up the phone and called the Manhattan branch of Team Jennifer. It was time to discuss clothing options.

Unfortunately, Jay wasn't home, and when I told my dad why I was calling, he just said, "Honey, you're so beautiful it doesn't matter what you wear." I wondered how many dads in America were, at that very moment, giving their daughters the same useless advice mine was giving me.

For different reasons, Martha and Clara were equally unhelpful.

"You should definitely wear a skirt," said Martha. "You have great legs." We were on a three-way call, each of us in front of her closet in case I needed to supplement with something from one of their wardrobes.

"Do *not* wear a skirt," said Clara. "He'll think you're one of those girls who wear skirts."

"Hey, *I* wear skirts," said Martha.

"Yes, but you *are* one of those girls who wears skirts," said Clara.

"What's *that* supposed to mean?"

"It *means* that you liked it when Todd gave you that stuffed duck, and Jenny would hate something like that."

Martha sounded really surprised. "You *would*?"

"I wouldn't *hate* it," I said. I didn't want Martha to be embarrassed about how happy she'd been when Todd gave her the duck on their one-month anniversary, especially since, objectively, the duck was completely cute and not annoying, like most stuffed animals.

Clara snorted, but I just said, "I think there are other things that are maybe more me." I thought of the fake profile Max had made me for my birthday. Was *that* me? Or was it just the fact that it had come from Max that had made it so perfect? If Max had given me, say, a stuffed bear holding a heart that said, *I wuv you beary*

201

much, would I have liked it as much as the funny, sarcastic article? Or was it impossible that I would ever even *like* a guy who would give me something like that?

"So what do *you* think she should wear?" asked Martha. Her question brought me back to the current crisis.

"*I* don't know," said Clara. "Jeans?"

"But what if he wants to take her to a fancy restaurant?"

Thinking about going out to a fancy restaurant with Gene made me need to sit down on the floor of my closet.

"Guys, this conversation is giving me a heart attack," I said.

"No way," said Clara. "A fancy restaurant is not 'random but cool.' He's taking her ice-skating or something."

"On the Lower East Side? Okay, you guys are officially useless," I said. "I'm hanging up now."

I put down the receiver and looked at the clothes hanging above me. If Gene went to private school in Manhattan which, given Jay and my dad's friends' demographics, he almost definitely did, then he was used to ultrachic Manhattan girls who wore clothes that had, like, been made for them *personally* by designers. He'd expect me to show up at 140 Ludlow Street in Manolo Blahnik heels and a tiny Zac Posen dress that I could wear to both the chic French bistro where we'd be eating *and* the private club at which we'd be seeing Manhattan's hottest performance artist commit unspeakable acts with her pet ferret.

Clearly, no matter how hard Martha and Clara and I worked to put together an acceptable outfit from our respective wardrobes, we were never going to make it happen.

In other words, what I needed to do was convince my mom to take me shopping.

♥ ♥ ♥

I never actually uttered the words "Jimmy Choo" or "haute couture" when I suggested to my mother that she and I should go to the White Plains Mall Friday after school, but I hoped once she saw me looking insanely foxy in some completely glam outfit, she wouldn't mind its ten-thousand-dollar price tag.

On Friday my mom asked if I'd mind meeting her at Donna's office even if it was a little bit out of the way, since the two of them were meeting to have "a talk" there. I wondered if their "talk" had something to do with my mom's going for drinks after the last few book club meetings (i.e., who she was going for drinks *with*). Having begrudged my mother her romance with Dr. Green when Max first dumped me for Anya, I was feeling a lot more generous about it now that I had a potential new boyfriend. It seemed to me that what Donna needed was not "a talk" with her best friend but perhaps "a date" with a stranger.

When I got to Donna's, the door to her inner-office was closed, and through the glass wall I could see that she and my mom were in the middle of a pretty intense-looking conversation.

I chatted for a minute with Sally, Donna's secretary, but her phone kept ringing, and it's kind of annoying to try to have a conversation when every two seconds the person has to say, "Excuse me a minute, hon. Hello, Donna Miller Realtors."

On the wall were pictures of houses in Hillsdale, and I walked over to check them out, wondering if I'd recognize any. None was familiar to me even though I figured I must have passed at least some of them, since Hillsdale is only about three square miles and I've lived here all my life. Houses in other towns were pictured, too, and on a lot of those listings, underneath the description of the house's "Greek Revival facade," "luxurious master bedroom suite," or "stainless steel chef's kitchen," in big block letters it invariably said HILLSDALE SCHOOL DISTRICT.

I went back and sat down in one of the chairs by the door. On the windowsill were two pamphlet dispensers, one on "Historic Hillsdale" and one featuring an article from a January issue of the *New York Times*'s real estate section, the title of which was "Hillsdale, NY: Hip, Hot, and Homey." I almost laughed out loud. Hillsdale was about as hip as my nana.

"Sooo, are you still seeing that cute boy you came in here with last time?" I looked up. Sally had her hands folded under her chin and was smiling, as if she hadn't just eviscerated me.

"Um, no. We broke up, actually." Her smile disappeared, immediately replaced by a look of genuine concern. I'm always amazed when people can do that. My response to bad news is always *totally* inappropriate. Like, I was running errands with my mother last year, and when we stopped at the dry cleaners, the woman there asked me how school was going and I gave her this polite smile and said it was going okay, and then my mom asked the woman how her husband was and the woman said, "Not so well, actually, he has cancer." And after she said it, I realized I *still* had the little smile on my face. I'd forgotten to send the message to my mouth, *Okay, time to turn down the corners of those lips now*, so it seemed like I was smiling at the news that her husband had *cancer*.

"Oh, my," said Sally. "What happened?"

The phone rang in the middle of her question,

which was no doubt a good thing, since I didn't think my saying *He dumped me for a retard* would exactly endear me to Sally. I grabbed a copy of the *New York Times* article, hoping if Sally finished her call and looked up to see me reading, she'd leave me alone.

Hillsdale, New York: Hip, Hot, and Homey

by Anna Hendriksen, special to *The New York Times*

If you're looking to be a thirty-minute commute from Manhattan, you might want to consider Hillsdale, a leafy suburban oasis that many Manhattan transplants love precisely because they say it feels so "unsuburby." "Even though we hated the idea of leaving Manhattan and moving to the suburbs, we kind of had no choice," says Ken Appleby, who moved to Hillsdale, along with his wife and their three-year-old twins last August. "The city just got so expensive."

I heard Sally hang up the phone and forced myself to look completely enthralled by the article, despite its being even more boring than my pre-calc textbook.

To Appleby and his wife, Hilary Maser, Hillsdale was the perfect compromise. "I grew up in a typical all-white suburb in Connecticut, where you had to drive *everywhere*," says Ms. Maser. "So it was really appealing to me that Hillsdale is not only incredibly integrated for a New York suburb, it also has a beautiful town center we can walk to."

But perhaps most important to couples like the Appleby-Masers—what drives the market on the one-million-plus–dollar price tag most of the homes in Hillsdale carry—is the town's extraordinary school district, which boasts some of the state's highest reading scores and more National Merit Scholars per capita than any other school in the state. The graduating classes are small (usually just over a hundred students), and the school feels more like an exclusive private academy than a public institution.

"It's not an exaggeration to say that Hillsdale's elementary school, junior high, and high school stand as examples of all that is great in public education," says Dr. Eric Thomas, Hillsdale's Superintendent of Schools. And the town's residents couldn't agree more.

Suddenly I didn't have to feign my interest in the article.

"Private school in Manhattan is *so* pricey," says Julie Curry, another recent transplant. "But you hear all these terrible stories about suburban schools—there's no diversity, there's no intellectual life, the only thing the kids care about is getting a BMW for graduation. But Hillsdale isn't like that. I was paying twenty-five thousand dollars a year for my daughter to go to private school, and I would be hard-pressed to find a way in which her education there was superior to the education she's getting at Hillsdale."

Doth the lady protest too much? If so, she's not alone. Other residents praise the area's superb restaurants, art house cinema, independent bookstores . . .

But I'd stopped reading. My heart was pounding, and when I looked up from the page, it took me a second to realize that my mother had walked out of Donna's office and was calling my name.

"Ready?" she asked when she saw she'd gotten my attention.

"Um, actually, I think I need to take a rain check."

My mom looked concerned. "What's wrong?" she asked.

"Nothing," I said, standing up, "but I think I just followed the money." And I ran out of the office, taking the article with me.

EIGHTEEN

· · ·

THE TENTH COMMANDMENT—GO FISH!

TODD AND I SPENT ALL Saturday writing the article. We worked from my house, and what with Todd making calls and saying, "Can I quote you on that?" my typing frantically, Clara Googling stuff like "top public high schools in America," and Martha running out for coffee and sandwiches, it felt like we were real reporters working on a real newspaper. My mom, Dr. Green, and Danny, newly freed from his cast, came in just after five, and I noticed that my brother chilled out in front of Todd, just saying, "Hi" and offering his hand for Todd to shake rather than slapping himself in the chest twice, making the black power salute and saying, "What up, bro?" which is his more typical greeting. He even asked (using a complete sentence *of grammatically correct English*) what we were working on and actually listened while I explained what the article was about.

I made a mental note to ask my mom if he'd gotten hit in the head with the puck during his game.

♥ ♥ ♥

It would be a lie to say I *completely* forgot about my date with Gene (especially since Jay texted me around noon to ask if I wanted to have dinner with them before my date, then my dad texted me two hours later to say they'd realized I wasn't coming over until *after* the date, then Jay texted me a *second* time to apologize for having texted me in the first place), but since I'd expected to spend Saturday morning huddled under the covers, paralyzed by anxiety, and Saturday afternoon puking (with a few minutes left to get dressed before I walked out the front door), the fact that I spent the whole day more or less completely focused on something that had nothing to do with the countdown to Gene seemed like a pretty significant accomplishment. Todd and I worked up to the last second, so I barely had time to take a shower, throw on a short black dress, and make it to a later train than the one I'd originally planned on taking, much less freak out in anticipation of my evening. I didn't even get to spend the train ride obsessing about the date because Todd called me from his house in a panic, thinking he'd just deleted the final draft of the article, and I had to listen to him read most of the document that he hadn't deleted before we realized he'd only deleted an earlier draft.

The train was packed and slow, so I was already running late by the time I got onto the subway. Then I had to figure out how to switch from the Six train to the F train, which I'd never done, and then I got totally turned around exiting the Second Avenue subway stop and ended up walking the wrong way on Houston, practically ending up in Jersey. When I finally turned onto Ludlow Street, rather than feeling relief, I experienced a brief moment of panic. Only, it was caused not by the fact that I was about to spend an evening with a complete stranger but by the sudden realization that I was fulfilling Dr. Emerson's tenth commandment (go on a date), having completely skipped her ninth (embrace change!).

Did I risk being struck by lightning for my blasphemous act?

But I was too busy trying not to freeze my ass off to worry about that, what with my having been taken in by the smiling little crocuses and daffodils that had shimmered in my sunny front yard all afternoon. Now that the temperature had dropped with the sun, I was wishing I'd worn a little black parka instead of a little black dress, and the prospect of being incinerated by a bolt of lightning didn't exactly fill me with dread.

At least I'd be warm.

And then, just as my underdressed, vaguely lost, running-late self walked by the third building on Ludlow Street that didn't have a number on it, I looked across the street and saw Eugene, standing next to a small, red neon sign that said ONE HUNDRED FORTY.

He *was* tall, probably six feet, and he was leaning comfortably against the wall, like waiting to spend the evening with someone he'd never met before was the most natural thing in the world. As I made my way across the street, he saw me, stepped away from the wall, and started walking in my direction.

His hair was a little darker and longer than it had been in the picture. He had on a pair of jeans and a dark green sweater, and his shoes were chocolate-brown suede.

My teeth started chattering, and not just from the cold.

"Hey," he said. "You're Jennifer." His smile was even better in real life.

"I'm Jennifer," I said. I wanted him to see how cute I looked in my little black dress, but I was so cold I couldn't help rubbing my arms, which kind of spoiled the effect.

"You must be freezing," he said, taking my hand. His fingers were warm, and I liked how he held mine—gently, but like he wasn't going to let go.

I followed him through the door he'd been leaning against, expecting to enter a dimly lit restaurant or maybe even a theater.

Instead, I found myself standing at the edge of a small square in a Spanish town. The stucco walls were decorated with trompe l'oeil drawings of shops and trees, streetlamps and a fountain and, in the distance, mountains and sky. Colored lights were draped along the beamed ceiling between intricately laced faux vines, and there were wrought-iron tables and chairs scattered around the edge of a dance floor that took up most of the room. Along one side of the dance floor, across the room from us, was a stage where a band was setting up. A bunch of the tables already had people sitting at them; some looked like college kids, some were more like my parents age and some seemed even older, like Nana. A few people were dressed in fancy clothes—suits and long dresses, but most were dressed more like Gene and I were.

Still holding my hand, he led me to a table not far from where the band was.

"Okay, it's possible you're going to think this is *incredibly* cheesy," he said.

"I don't know, I like it so far," I said. The room was warm and there was the hum of conversation. A waitress dressed like a Spanish dancer, with a rose behind her ear, came over to our table.

"Could we have a pitcher of sangria?" Gene asked. Then he turned to me. "Sorry, is that okay with you?"

"Sure," I said. I wasn't sure what sangria was. I hoped it wasn't some gross type of alcohol. I'm okay with wine and beer, but if Gene had just ordered us something with, say, Jägermeister in it, I was screwed.

When the waitress left, he observed, "I think they would serve my little sister here." Then he added, "She's twelve."

I considered mentioning my younger brother as per Martha's suggestion but decided to hold Danny in reserve in case conversation looked bleak later in the evening.

"Sorry I was late," I said. "I meant to take an earlier train, but the day kind of got away from me."

Gene nodded. "I know the feeling," he said. "Let me guess—huge English essay?"

"That was yesterday," I said. "Today was major reportorial scoop."

"Oh, wow," he said. "What about?"

I started to tell him about the article. When I got to the part where I'd found the thing about housing costs and the school district, he said, "That's amazing!" and even though normally I'd downplay what I'd done, tonight I didn't want to. Gene didn't seem to think I was being conceited either, which was cool of him. When

the waitress came, he poured each of us a glass of sangria, and suddenly I realized something.

"Am I talking too much?" I asked.

"No," he said, and when I looked at him sus-
piciously he laughed and added, "Really."

Just as I finished telling him about editing the final
draft from the train, the band played a few notes and a
woman in a long black dress came to the middle of the
dance floor. Several of the couples who'd been sitting at
tables got up and stood around her.

"What's happening?" I asked. I took a sip of my sangria. It was sweet, and there were little pieces of fruit
floating around in it. It tasted kind of like juice, and I
took a big swig.

"Careful," said Gene, when I came up for air. He
pointed at my glass. "This has more alcohol than you'd
think."

I put my glass down. The last thing I needed was to
end the night puking onto Gene's brown suede shoes. I
gestured at the dance floor and asked my question again.
"What are they doing?" The woman was talking to the
people standing around her.

"Okay," said Gene. "This is the part where things
could head south." He took a deep breath, and I realized
he must have been a little nervous, too. "It's a salsa
lesson."

"Sorry?"

"Those people up there"—he pointed at the dance floor—"they're taking a salsa lesson."

"Oh," I said. "And we're going to watch them?"

"Not exactly," said Gene.

Either the sangria was even stronger than Gene thought or the stress of working on the article had done something to my brain.

"I'm not following you," I said.

Gene stood up. "We're taking a salsa lesson," he said.

I stayed sitting down. "Um, the thing is, I'm a lot better at talking than I am at dancing," I said.

"Me too," said Gene. But he didn't sit down. In fact, he took a step toward the dance floor and held out his hand to me. "Come on."

I stayed sitting. The only time I ever dance is when Martha and Clara and I blast ABBA and jump around. I'd never danced with a guy before, unless you count those slow dances at bar and bat mitzvahs when you just stand there with your arms around each other, not really moving, while everyone points and stares and says really stupid stuff like, "Get a room," even though you wouldn't know what to do with a room if you had one.

The smile was fading from Gene's face, and I could tell he was starting to regret his "kind of random but hopefully cool" plan for the evening. I tried putting myself in his place. Okay, imagine I'm trying to decide what to do with some girl from the suburbs I've never met. I reject dinner and a movie (too boring), bowling (too retro), a museum (too pretentious). Then I come up with this (objectively great) idea. A cool activity in a cool part of town. Only, my date just sits there.

As Gene, I started to ever so slightly hate me.

I stood up. "I have no rhythm whatsoever," I said.

"Me either," he said.

"I'll probably step on your toes," I said.

"Oh, I'll *definitely* step on yours," he said.

The teacher, Marabelle, was lining everyone up, the men facing the women. Gene got on the end of the men's line, and I got on the end of the women's, facing him, and then Marabelle came and stood with her back to the women and showed us the step we were supposed to do, calling it something like "step—fall—change"; fall, in my case, being the operative word. I kept putting my left foot down when I was supposed to be putting my right foot down, and I always seemed to have one extra step to go in order to get the foot that was supposed to be starting the next cycle to the place it was supposed to be starting the next cycle from.

Luckily, Gene hadn't been lying—when Marabelle started demonstrating for the guys, I watched him do a bunch of quick moves not unlike mine to get his feet where they were supposed to be. The woman next to me was mumbling to herself; she wasn't much better than I had been, which was a relief. In fact, as far as I could tell, most of us pretty much sucked.

We got to practice on our own for a long time, the men working on their steps, the women working on ours. Once Marabelle came over to me and tried to show me what I was doing wrong, but even though she kept assuring me that, "Eet is as natural as walking," I think by the end of my mini private lesson, I'd done more to shake her confidence than she had to boost mine.

By nine o'clock, the room was a lot more crowded than it had been when we'd arrived, and there was a whole band set up on the stage. I'd been looking at my feet for so long I was surprised to see that dozens of people had arrived, many more of them than before dressed in fancy clothes. I looked over at Gene, who was staring at his shoes, trying to master the third step Marabelle had taught us. He got it once, then tried it again and totally screwed up. But when he looked up at me he was smiling, like he didn't mind that he wasn't very good.

Marabelle clapped her hands, thanked us for our hard work, and said we could find her all evening if we had any questions. Then she excused herself, the band started playing, and a minute later the floor was full of couples dancing. Except for those of us who had been at the lesson, everyone knew how to dance. A couple swept by, executing a complicated version of one of the steps we'd just learned. I watched the woman's delicate footwork, her high-heeled shoes seeming to move of their own accord. Her partner held her lightly in his arms, his upper body stiff, just like Marabelle had showed us, his hips moving smoothly back and forth like hers.

I was pretty sure there wasn't enough sangria in the world to enable me to do that.

Gene came over to where I was standing. I realized my jaw had been hanging open as I watched the dancers go by, and I shut it quickly. He nodded at the couple that had just passed us.

"I figure we'll look like that," he said. "Maybe a little better."

"Oh, no doubt," I said, looking up at him. He really *was* handsome, and when he put his hand on my waist and took my hand, it felt surprisingly comfortable, even though I was now standing in the arms of someone I had met all of an hour ago. The music was so good it was impossible *not* to move your hips and your feet. The problem was we had no idea *how* to move them, so we kept getting hopelessly tangled up in one another. The first time we did a full body bump I was totally embarrassed, but we did it so many more times it was hard to stay embarrassed. We circled around the floor, and each time one of the really good couples passed us, Gene stood up perfectly straight, like the man, and I arched my back and twitched my hips, like the woman, but then we would start cracking up and it would be impossible to take another step until we caught our breath. Finally Gene said, "Do you want to get some dinner before we do serious injury to ourselves?" and I said yes.

We went back to our table, and when the waitress came over, we both ordered quesadillas. It was weird how I wasn't nervous anymore, but maybe if you trip over somebody's feet enough times, it's hard to feel self-conscious around him.

"This was a great idea," I said, looking around the beautiful room at the graceful couples sweeping past us. "Thank you."

Over dinner, we talked about our school papers. Gene (who *did* go to private school) said his had gotten better but was still taken up mostly with school gossip (like who was going out with whom) and an advice column that was full of private jokes nobody but the writer and her friends got. I told him about the *Spectator* and how it mostly focused on non-Hillsdale stuff because the editor in chief thought that was important. It felt weird to talk about Max as the editor in chief, as if our only relationship was the one we had from working on the paper together. But I guess now it kind of was.

"Is that what you'll keep the focus on, if you're editor in chief next year? Non-school-related stuff?" Gene asked.

"I don't know," I said. And then I admitted to Gene what I hadn't been able to admit to Todd the day he and I had talked about my possibly becoming editor in chief of the *Spectator* next year. "The thing is, that kind of stuff isn't really reporting, you know? It's more, like, a Spark Notes of what real newspapers are saying. Doing this article made me see that reporting on what's happening at Hillsdale is actually more like being a real reporter than reporting on stuff that real reporters are reporting on." I knew I'd put my answer in kind of convoluted terms and I looked up at him. "Does that make sense?"

"Absolutely," he said, nodding. "You're the one in the trenches."

"Exactly," I said. And even though my next question was a complete non sequitur, I couldn't not ask it. Gene was just too nice and too cute and too funny. Something was definitely wrong. "Can I ask you something?"

"Shoot," he said.

"How come you don't have a girlfriend?" I'd meant my question as a compliment, but I blurted it out so abruptly it sounded more like an accusation.

"How come you don't have a boyfriend?" he countered.

I felt my cheeks get hot. "We broke up," I said.

"So did we," said Gene. Then he said, "Sorry, I didn't mean to sound defensive. It's just"—he looked up at the ceiling and laughed briefly at some private joke before looking back at me—"I think part of the reason Jay was so desperate to fix us up is because of how much he and my parents *hated* my last girlfriend."

"*Really?* Why?" I was intrigued. I mean, my mom wasn't exactly president of the Max Brown Fan Club, but I wouldn't say she'd *hated* him.

Gene shook his head. "She was kind of high maintenance," he said. "You know, very Upper-East-Side heiress type." I pictured an extremely thin girl with angular hair and stilettos riding to and from Barneys in her limo.

"The funny thing is," Gene said, chewing thoughtfully on a piece of ice, "I would probably have broken up with her even sooner than I did if they hadn't wanted me to break up with her so badly. It was a little perverse. You know, like, *I'll show you*. Only, the joke was on me because she was such a *complete* pain in the ass. Not

222

to bad-mouth her," he added quickly. For a second I wondered if he'd read Dr. Emerson, but it seemed unlikely. I couldn't quite picture Gene taping Girlfriend, you are number one! to his bathroom mirror.

He shrugged. "Anyway, long story short, a while ago I had to write this application for an internship, and she went kind of crazy because I couldn't go to a party this girl we know was having in the Hamptons, and blah blah blah, we had a huge fight and that was that.

"Sorry," he said, pouring me some more sangria, "I didn't mean to go on and on about the whole thing. It's really no big deal." He put the pitcher down on the table and took a sip from his glass. "How about you?"

I should have figured he was going to ask, but some-how I was totally unprepared for the question. "Oh, I—" After Gene's story, I just couldn't bring myself to admit that Max had dumped me for somebody else.

"Don't want to talk about it?" asked Gene, finishing my sentence.

"Kind of," I said.

He nodded. "Yeah, I had one of those," he said.

The waitress came by and asked if we wanted dessert, and we agreed to split a flan, and for the rest of the meal we didn't talk about our breakups, we just talked. Maybe because he already knew Jay and my dad so well, Gene really didn't feel like a stranger—more like an old friend of the family's. Which I guess he was. Regardless, the awkwardness I'd expected never materialized, and by the time I told him about Danny referring to the girls in his class as being in need of "a little Danny luv," I was just telling the story because it was funny, not because we'd run out of things to talk about.

And then suddenly, it was twelve thirty. People were still dancing, and the club was even more packed than it had been earlier, but everyone there looked a little old for a curfew.

"I should probably get home," I said. I'd promised my dad and Jay I'd be at their apartment by one.

Gene gestured for the check, and when I reached for my wallet, he said, "I'll get it."

"You don't have to," I said.

"You can get it next time," he said. And when he said it I got this unexpected tingly feeling. *He wants there to be a next time.*

Outside it was even colder than it had been before, and I started shivering right away. "Wait a sec," said Gene. "Let me give you my sweater."

I turned to him, about to say something totally inane like, *You don't have to*, but then he took a step toward me and I took a step toward him and suddenly we had our arms around each other and were kissing. For a split second it felt amazing—his lips were gentle and he tasted like the orange slices that had been in the sangria. I put my hand on the back of his head and felt his hair, twisting it between my fingers.

And then something happened. I don't know if it was touching his hair or his hands on the small of my back or just the fact that I was kissing somebody new, but all of a sudden I missed Max so much I couldn't breathe. I'd always thought it was a metaphor when people talked about being brokenhearted, but standing there, kissing Gene, I felt my heart split in two. It was a physical pain; before I knew it my eyes had filled up with tears and I'd pulled away.

"I'm really sorry," I said, but I don't think he could understand me since I was crying so hard.

"Are you okay?" Gene asked. I'd turned away from him, and he put his hand on my shoulder and tried to turn me around.

"No, please," I said. "I have to——" God, could this be any more embarrassing? My nose was running and I could barely catch my breath. I spotted an empty cab heading toward us, and without saying anything to Gene, I stepped out into the street. The cab came to a screeching halt inches from me.

"Jennifer?" Gene said as I fumbled for the door of the cab. I knew I was being totally rude, but I also knew my face was covered in snot and tears and mascara, and his seeing me was more horrible than his thinking I had no manners.

"It's nothing you did," I said. "I just have to go. I'm really sorry." Gene touched my back.

"Jennifer?" he asked again.

"Please," I said. "Just let me go." I finally got the door open and practically fell into the cab swiping at my face with the back of my arm and slamming the door shut behind me. The driver pulled away from the curb as quickly as he'd stopped, and for a second I wondered what conclusions he'd draw about the scene he was witnessing. But really I didn't care what he thought. I just wanted to be home.

"Where to, Miss?" he asked.

"Grand Central," I managed to choke out. I'd call my dad and Jay from the train, tell them I'd decided to go home. Thinking about taking the train back to Westchester made me think about Max and all the times we'd taken the train from the city late at night. Even though it had been over two months since we'd broken up, and probably more like three since we'd been in Manhattan together, it felt like yesterday, like I could open the cab door onto January and Max.

How were you ever supposed to get over someone if you never felt time was passing, if it always felt like you'd just broken up? I'd done everything I was supposed to do. I'd followed all the rules. And *still* the idea that I'd never kiss Max again made me so sad I couldn't breathe. It wasn't fair.

It wasn't fair.

When I got home at a little after two, I was so tired I just wanted to collapse into bed. But there was one thing I had to do first. I went upstairs and opened my night table. There was *The Breakup Bible*. I took it out of the drawer and brought it downstairs.

Then I went outside, opened the garbage can, and tossed it in.

NINETEEN

• • •

CONGRATULATIONS! YOU'VE GONE FROM HEARTACHE TO HAPPINESS!

I FELT AS IF I'D BEEN running and running as fast as I could up the longest, steepest mountain in the world, only to find, when I arrived at the top, that what awaited me there was a brick wall into which I slammed, face-first.

I barely even read the e-mail Gene sent me early Sunday morning. "Sorry last night didn't work out. Hope you got home okay. Good luck with the article." I mean, what was I supposed to write back? No, *I'm* sorry, Gene. I'm sorry I'm a huge loser who's *still in love with the ex-boyfriend who just celebrated his two-month anniversary with his new girlfriend.*

On Monday afternoon when I walked into the *Spectator* meeting, Max was sitting at a computer

228

with his back to the door. I couldn't help staring at him, trying to figure out what his secret was. It was like he had some kind of magical power over me— I looked at him, and the rational part of my brain thought, *You should not care about this person.* But then I thought about him being with Anya, and I got that ache in my chest, and suddenly I couldn't catch my breath. If only there were a switch to turn off the boy-liking part of my brain. I wouldn't have minded never falling in love again, spending the rest of my life alone, if it meant I wouldn't be sad about Max any-more.

As if he could sense my thinking about him, Max turned in my direction. I felt my cheeks blaze and I looked away.

Mr. Barton walked in a few minutes late, carrying a stack of xeroxes, which he passed around to everyone sitting at the table. When he got to me, I was surprised to see that what he was distributing was Todd's and my article.

"Okay," said Mr. Barton, when Leslie, who'd rushed in later even than Mr. Barton, had taken her seat. "I want everyone to take a minute to read the article Todd and Jennifer wrote."

There was silence. It was a little embarrassing to sit there while everyone read something I'd written. Not sure what to do with my eyes, I ended up just reading along with everyone else.

Hillsdale, New York: Hip, Hot, and Hypocritical

by Todd Kincaid and Jennifer Lewis

Hillsdale is one of the hottest suburbs in the New York metropolitan area for a number of reasons: proximity to Manhattan (just thirty minutes by train), beautiful homes (some with views of the water), and a school district that's routinely named one of the fifty best in the country by *USA Today*. But if newcomers and old-timers alike praise the community for these and other attributes, there is a darker side to the Hillsdale school system that is rarely addressed in public. Despite having an African American population that makes up nearly twenty percent of the student body, this twenty percent is largely excluded from the school's most demanding curriculum.

"I go to see the basketball team or the football team, and you'd think we have a school that's ninety percent black," says Alex Martin, an African American member of this year's junior class. "Then I look around my AP history class and there's not one other black face in it."

Though the school's administration insists, "Race is not a factor in determining eligibility for AP classes," there's no denying very few minority students find themselves taking college-level courses. "My inclusion class is *all* black," says Tiffany King, a sophomore. "Why?"

Segregation isn't restricted to the classroom, however. Check out the cafeteria next time you're there, and you'll see tables of black students and tables of white students (though many of the white students will probably be dressed in fashions made popular by African American rappers). "You've never seen so many kids be so white and act so black," observed Rafat Smith as she described a typical lunch period. "It's like, they don't want to *hang out* with black kids, but they sure want to look like us."

A request to poll the student body about some of these issues was refused by the school's administration. Mr. Michaels expressed concern that such a survey would "create" racial tensions where they don't exist, and Superintendent Thomas pointed out that race is a "volatile subject."

According to Donna Miller, a realtor in Hillsdale, "The idea that they will be sending their children to an exemplary school district where they will encounter a diverse population is a major selling point" for potential Hillsdale residents. In an informal poll of her fellow brokers, Ms. Miller found that almost all of their clients would be disturbed to discover how segregated the school is, even if that segregation is *de facto* and not *de jure*.

Are issues of race and diversity adequately addressed at Hillsdale High? Let us know your thoughts at letters@thespectator.org.

"What's *de facto*?" asked Leslie.

"'In fact,'" I said. "*De jure* is by law."

She shook her head to indicate she still didn't get what I meant.

"We're saying it's not *legal* segregation; it's just how things work out."

"Wow," said Malcolm. He looked from me to Todd and then back again. "Is this all true?"

"It's true," said Todd. He took his notebook out of his pocket and waved it briefly. "I've got the notes to back it up."

"This is intense," said Anya. I wanted not to care that she was impressed by what we'd written, what with my hating her so much, but I couldn't help but like the fact that I'd amazed even someone as ditzy as Anya.

"Yes, Ms. Cates, it *is* intense," agreed Mr. Barton. "And we're going to take some flak for it. Which is why before we run it, I want the editorial board to have a chance to criticize or question or even kill any aspect of the article you don't feel you can stand behind."

"What do you mean by 'flak'?" asked Sarah.

"I mean that the administration is not going to be happy about the article. They're not going to be happy with me. They're not going to be happy with you."

"You mean, like, they could fire you?" asked Anya.

Mr. Barton shrugged. "Why don't we decide

whether or not we think we can stand behind this article for its own sake before we get caught up in a lot of hypothetical consequences," he said.

"Hell, I don't care if they *like* me," said Malcolm. "I don't exactly like them." Freshman year, Malcolm got suspended for (as he tells it) calling a girl stupid. My guess is the situation was probably a little more complicated than his version of the story would imply, but regardless, he's never forgiven Mr. Michaels.

Still, I felt a little uneasy about how vague Dr. Barton was being. Could they really *fire* him?

Gordon was nodding at what Malcolm had said. "I think this is a really good article," he said. "I'd be psyched to see it run."

"Me too," said Leslie.

"Ditto," said Sarah.

"Totally," said Anya.

"Mr. Brown?" said Mr. Barton.

Max hesitated, but I had the feeling it wasn't Mr. Barton's future he was thinking about. He looked around the table, carefully avoiding meeting my eyes. His shoulders slumped a little, but his voice was confident. "Sure," he said. "Of course we should run it."

"I'm happy to hear that," he said. "Now, let the games begin."

For the next hour, the room was a hive of activity.

Everyone was either printing or editing or photoshopping sections of the May issue. Personally, I was glad for the distraction. People kept coming up to me and saying how good they thought the article was, but I couldn't stop thinking about what Mr. Barton had said. I mean, it's one thing to have Mr. Michaels mad at me (something I'd managed to accomplish without the article even getting published). It was another thing to get my favorite teacher fired.

At the end of the meeting, I lingered after everyone had gone.

"What's on your mind, Lewis?" asked Mr. Barton.

I considered beating around the bush, asking Mr. Barton to elaborate on what he'd meant by "hypothetical consequences." But then I rejected the idea. What if Mr. Barton thought I was worried about Max not getting to be valedictorian? I decided to be straight. "In the meeting, when Anya asked if they could fire you, you didn't say no," I said.

"And?" said Mr. Barton.

"And . . . I want to know if you really think that's a possibility."

"Why?" asked Mr. Barton.

"*Why?*" I repeated, incredulous. When he didn't answer me, I stated the obvious. "Because I don't want you to lose your job."

Mr. Barton stared at me, tapping his finger against his lips. "You want to be a reporter, right?" he said.

I nodded.

"And you want to be a really good reporter. You don't want to cover beauty pageants in Des Moines, right?"

I nodded again.

"Okay, then." He grabbed his battered briefcase, slung the strap over his shoulder, and was out the door before I could say anything else.

TWENTY

* * *

WHAT HAVE WE LEARNED
FROM OUR BREAKUP?

"LOOK, IT'S HIS DECISION," said my dad. "He's a grown man, and if he believes it's worth risking his job for the article, that's a risk he's allowed to take."

We were sitting at Cantina, which is normally my favorite restaurant in Hillsdale, but I was too distracted by the fact that tomorrow was May 1st (D-Day) to do more than pick at my paella. Danny, however, suffered from no such loss of appetite, and upon finishing his entrée, he'd turned his attention to mine. For the past several minutes, his fork had been making steady trips between my plate and his mouth.

"I don't want to be editor in chief if someone else is advising the paper," I said. Suddenly I thought of something—what if *Mr. Michaels* became the new adviser?

236

Just remembering how much he disliked me made my stomach hurt. Not that the other alternatives were especially attractive. "What if they give it to Mr. Anthony?" Mr. Anthony is a history teacher who's obsessed with football. "We'll have to have, like, a twenty-page sports section."

"Ain't nothin' wrong with that," said Danny.

My dad looked at Danny. "You *do* know how to speak English properly, right? I mean, this isn't something I have to worry about, is it?"

"Chill, Dad," said Danny. "It's all cool."

My dad started to say something, but Jay gave him a look. Then he smiled at me. "So how are things going with Dr. Emerson?" he asked. Danny snorted, and I pushed his fork out of my plate.

"Hey!" he complained.

"Dr. Emerson is in the garbage can," I said. "Which is where she should have been from the beginning."

"Oh, I don't know," said Jay. "Some of her advice wasn't all bad. Just because things didn't work out with Gene . . ."

I held up my hand. "*Please*," I said. "Let us *never* speak of him. He thinks I'm a total freak."

"He doesn't think you're a freak," said Jay, shaking his head. "He really enjoyed your date."

Hearing the words "your date" in conjunction with Gene was enough to make me lose what little appetite I'd had. I pushed my plate over to Danny.

"I probably scarred him for life. He's like, girls— one second they're laughing at your jokes, the next second they're sobbing onto your face."

Danny practically choked on my paella. "You *sobbed* on his *face?*"

"It was a figure of *speech*," I said, my teeth clenched.

Jay took a sip of wine. "If it's any consolation, you didn't scar him for life. Last I heard, he was getting back together with his heiress." He rolled his eyes to indicate his feelings about the reconciliation.

"Oh," I said. Considering I'd just said I never wanted to hear Gene's name spoken in my presence again, the little flicker of sadness I felt on hearing Jay's news didn't exactly make sense.

"Now *there's* a man who knows what time it is," said Danny. "Gotta play the field."

"I think I'm going to have a heart attack," said my dad.

"Let's talk about something else," suggested Jay.

I couldn't have agreed more.

♥ ♥ ♥

The Spectator is distributed during homeroom, and since the article was on the front page above the fold, people didn't exactly have to search for it. By second period, when I was on my way to Spanish, everyone seemed to be talking about what Todd and I had written. Señora Hanover tried to conduct a discussion of a Borges story we'd read, but eventually she gave up and let the class discuss race relations at Hillsdale. The same thing happened in math, only it was linear equations we stopped talking about and the merits of a race-blind tracking system that we debated. In English we shelved *Heart of Darkness* to talk about why there weren't more African American writers in the honors curriculum. I noticed that Michael Hyde (who has an even more ridiculous *Yo, homey, what up?* routine than my brother) didn't say a word the whole class. When he stood up at the end of the period, he turned his baseball cap around so the bill was in the front, not the back.

On my way from English to history, I passed Todd standing with a group of black students. "Hey," he called to me.

"Hey," I called back. He said something to one of the guys he was standing with, and the guy smiled at me and said, "Nice article." The other people standing with them nodded.

"Thanks," I said, and as I was walking away I realized the guy who had just talked to me was *in my grade*. He was in my grade and we'd never spoken to each other.

How was it possible for anyone to claim there wasn't segregation at Hillsdale?

That in my head I was winning the argument with the administration didn't assuage the anxiety I felt when I passed the main office just in time to see Mr. Barton being ushered into Mr. Michaels's office.

♥ ♥ ♥

Clara and Martha wanted to take Todd and me out to lunch to celebrate the huge buzz our article had generated, but I couldn't go. In fact, I barely had time to run by the cafeteria and grab a sandwich since my lunch period would be spent not toasting my triumph but typing the seniors' last will and testaments. The final *Spectator* of the year is insanely annoying to produce— basically, we spend the entire month of May laying out the seniors' inane writing ("Hey, hey, J.J., whadda ya say? I'm totally gonna miss you, big guy!"). When we're not entering what they've "written," we're chasing down the ones who've neglected to turn in their behests—God forbid they regret for all eternity not having thanked their "buds" for "those *awesome* potato skins at TGIF!"

If you ask me, the graduation issue of the *Spectator* is the manifestation of everything that's wrong with the modern media.

Just as I was estimating how long it would take if I got on the line for sandwiches and debating whether I had time or should just grab something from the salad bar, I saw Max coming toward me from the other side of the cafeteria. My heart skipped a beat, and the noise of the lunchroom seemed to simultaneously recede and intensify, like I was walking through an echo chamber.

Had he liked the article? He hadn't said anything to me about it all week, but by now he *had* to be over any resentment he'd had about not coming up with the idea himself. And he had to be at least a little psyched that the *Spectator* was getting so much attention—normally, the only time you hear about the paper after it comes out is when teachers yell at students for leaving it lying around instead of putting it in the trash when they're done reading (or not reading) it.

I knew I shouldn't care what Max thought, but I couldn't help myself. I wanted him to say he was glad we'd run the piece, that he was . . . well, that he was impressed by what Todd and I had done.

He was walking fast enough that he was practically in front of me before he saw me. "Hi," I said. It was the first time I'd spoken directly to him in weeks.

He hesitated for a second, like he wasn't sure he was going to respond to me until he was actually doing it.

"Hi," he said. Then he stood there, as if he was waiting for me to say something else.

I couldn't bring myself to ask, *So, are you psyched about the article?* It was too much like fishing for a compliment. "Um, you haven't seen Mr. Barton, have you?" I asked instead. Maybe Max would know something about what had happened earlier today in Mr. Michaels's office.

But he shook his head. "Nope," he said. Then he smiled this totally fake smile and tapped me on the shoulder. "But hey, guess what—Mr. Michaels wants to see me later today. Guess he wants to talk to me about that article you wrote."

"Oh," I said. It wasn't like I could say, *Thanks*, since what he'd said wasn't exactly a compliment.

"Yeah," he said, the forced smile still plastered on. "You certainly found the perfect way to get me back, didn't you?"

"Get you back?" I repeated dumbly.

Max folded his arms and gave me a look like he was a teacher dealing with a particularly obtuse student. "Look, I'm really sorry I didn't tell you about Anya. But I didn't *purposely* set out to hurt you. It just happened. Which is more than I can say for—" He didn't finish the sentence, his implied *you* was enough.

"Is that what you think? That I wrote this article to

get back at you?" Obviously it *was* what he thought, what with his *saying* it and all, but the accusation was so outrageous I was sure I'd somehow misunderstood him.

He snorted, then made his voice high-pitched. "Oh, Jennifer's such a *brilliant* reporter. Oh, isn't she *fabulous*. You know, that *evil* editor Max Brown? I heard he tried to stop her from running the article. Doesn't he suck? Isn't he selfish? You know *all* he cares about is being valedictorian." Dropping his voice into its normal register, he said, "Well, you got what you wanted. You're the heroine. I'm the villain. Congratulations. Oh, and yeah, I *would* have liked to be valedictorian. But I guess you took care of that, too."

Suddenly I felt a cold wave of fury wash over me. I thought about all the hard work Todd and I had done, how exciting it had been when we finally got the story, how worried I was that Mr. Barton was going to get in trouble. The only time I *hadn't* thought about Max since we'd broken up was when I was working on the article. And now Max wanted to turn the whole thing into my way of getting revenge on him?

"You're an idiot, Max, you know that?" The words I spoke came spilling out of me almost faster than my mouth could form them. "I *never* wanted to hurt you, I *never* wanted to embarrass you, and I *really* couldn't care less if you're valedictorian. I pursued this article because

I thought it was a good idea, and if you knew the first thing about being a reporter *or* an editor, you'd have *known* it was a good idea. So I'm sorry you're so self-centered that all you can think about is how this story affects *you*." I turned and started to walk away, then turned back. Max was staring at me, his mouth a wide *O* of surprise. "Can I make an editorial suggestion? Get over yourself."

I marched out of the cafeteria, so mad I didn't even stop to get something to eat.

♥ ♥ ♥

The fact that Mr. Barton didn't show up in the *Spectator* office Tuesday afternoon only increased my anxiety about his meeting with Mr. Michaels. I sent him an e-mail at the *Spectator*'s Gmail account, but he didn't get back to me. By third period Wednesday, my sense of foreboding had metastasized into something that felt a lot like panic.

On my way to math I decided that if I couldn't find Mr. Barton by lunch, I was going to barge into Mr. Michaels's office and demand to know what had happened between him and Mr. Barton. Just as I was writing the lead in my head for my article on the need for a *serious* overhaul of the school's administration, there was a tap on my shoulder and I turned around.

"Mr. Barton!" I was so relieved to see him I could have cried. "What happened?"

"Reporter Lewis," he said, holding out his hand. "My congratulations."

His tone was serious, almost somber. I took his hand numbly and we shook. He gestured with his head in the direction of Mr. Michaels's office. "I've had a veritable cornucopia of meetings," he said. "I just came from one now, in fact. You should know that Mr. Michaels has been getting a lot of phone calls from parents. They're not too happy."

It was like all the blood rushed from my head to my feet. The edges of my vision grew blurry.

Mr. Barton continued. "It seems they want to know why up to now there's been no forum for a discussion of racial issues at Hillsdale and to express their happiness that Mr. Michaels, Dr. Thomas, the staff of the paper, and I have sought to rectify the situation."

"What?!" I couldn't believe it. "But Mr. Michaels and Dr. Thomas were totally *against* talking about race."

Mr. Barton laughed. "Never underestimate the power of the hegemony to co-opt that which would threaten said hegemony," he said.

"Okay, I have *no* idea what you just said," I admitted.

"Let's just say Mr. Michaels knows the cardinal rule of dealing with troublemakers."

"Which is?" I asked.

"If you can't beat 'em, join 'em." He chuckled to himself. "I hope to see more of this kind of reporting next year, Ms. Lewis," he said. "Or should I say, Editor in Chief Lewis?"

I opened my mouth to say something to him, but no words came out. He gave me a two-fingered salute and turned to head down the hall. By the time I'd managed to stutter a *Thank you*, he'd already turned the corner and disappeared from sight, and I didn't want to go bounding after him like some hyperactive cheerleader.

Instead I just stood there, feeling something I hadn't felt in a long time.

Happy.

♥ ♥ ♥

My happiness was short-lived. When I got home from school, there was an envelope addressed to me with the return address of *The New York Times*. The envelope was thin, like it had exactly one piece of paper in it, which, as anyone who knows anyone who's applied to college knows, is bad news. Rejection letters are thin. Acceptance letters are fat. I stood there holding my thin envelope, starting to get mad all over again. Only, this time I wasn't mad at Max, I was mad at myself. *Why* had I let my feelings for him get in the way of writing a

246

really great essay for the *Times*? Why had I spent that weekend reading the stupid *Breakup Bible* instead of doing something that would really matter to me? The whole situation was enough to make me want to give myself a swift kick in the ass, which, unfortunately, is more or less physically impossible.

I shrugged. "Whatever," I said out loud, even though there was no one else around to hear me. Then I ripped open the envelope, trying to distract myself from my disappointment by making a mental wager on whether the letter would begin, *We are sorry to inform you . . .* or *Unfortunately, we were unable to . . .* I decided on the latter, then unfolded the thick, white paper.

Dear Ms. Lewis: On behalf of The New York Times*, it is my pleasure to inform you that you have been offered a summer internship. . . .*

I didn't start jumping up and down, screaming my head off. And I didn't pick up the phone to call everyone I knew and tell them. Instead I stood there, feeling for the tiny bud of happiness that had poked its head out when Mr. Barton told me I was going to be the paper's next editor in chief.

It was still there.

TWENTY-ONE

. . .

MAKE YOURS THE LIFE YOU WANT!

IT WAS LIKE THE UNIVERSE was in on the good news about my internship; the warm, breezy evening was perfect for eating out on the back deck, which we almost never do. Even Danny could feel the night's specialness—he actually put his napkin on his lap and complimented Mom on her cooking. We finished our dinner just as the sun set in a riotous explosion of color that seemed to kiss the smooth wooden table.

"Listen," said my mom, fishing a mushroom out of the salad bowl. "Don't freak out, but Nana wants to throw a dinner party in your honor."

I spoke without swallowing the piece of garlic bread I'd just popped in my mouth, so my "Why?" came out fairly garbled.

248

"To celebrate!" she said, ignoring my poor table manners and raising her glass of iced tea in my direction. "Your article. The internship. We'll invite your dad and Jay and Martha and Todd and Clara and Donna."

I made a face. So did Danny, who calls Donna *Le Witch*.

"*And Donna*," my mother repeated. "Donna, who made it possible for you to write that wonderful article. Donna, to whom I know you feel a debt of gratitude too great ever to be repaid."

"Fine," I said, stabbing at my last bite of chicken. "Point taken. We can invite Donna."

"What about your *boyfriend*?" said Danny. "What about"—he made his voice dreamy and clasped his hands together in front of his chest—"*Ev-an?*"

"Daniel, don't you have somewhere to be?" my mom asked.

"Always," he said, standing up. I noticed he was wearing Dad's Wesleyan sweatshirt. "Hey!" I said. "That's mine!"

"Chill out," he said. "You can have it back if it's so precious." He went to take it off, but I made a face.

"Thanks, I'll wait till it's been washed, if you don't mind."

Danny shrugged. "Suit yourself," he said. "Later." He headed into the kitchen.

"Dishes!" my mom yelled. As my brother headed

into the kitchen, this time carrying his plate and fork, I noticed something else about him.

"Do those jeans actually *fit* you?" Normally when Danny walks away you get to enjoy about half of his boxer-clad butt hanging out of his pants.

Danny looked over his shoulder at his ass. "Hey, if you've got it, flaunt it," he said. Then he went inside.

"I think your article really had an impact on him," said my mom, as we gathered up the utensils and collected them on the empty chicken platter.

"*My article*? I didn't even know he read it."

She nodded. "I overheard him on the phone saying it was uncool to 'be so white and dress so black.'"

"Wow," I said, smiling to myself.

"There you have it," she said. "The power of the press right in your very own home." She stood up and started stacking the remaining dishes. I stood up, too, but then I realized there was something I needed to say, and I sat back down again.

"Mom?" She'd already taken a few steps toward the kitchen, but when she saw I was sitting, she came back to the table.

"Yeah?"

"I'm glad about you and Dr. Green," I said.

My mom put down the dishes she'd been carrying. Then she bent over and gave me a hug.

"Thanks, honey," she said. "That means a lot to me. I know you're going to like Evan. He's just the greatest guy."

I hoped she wasn't about to start enumerating Dr. Evan Green's myriad attributes. I didn't mind her *being* into some guy, but I didn't have to listen to her *share* how into him she was, did I?

She stroked my hair, a thoughtful expression on her face. "Any chance that boy you went on a date with might want to come to your dinner?"

"*Gene?*" A shudder of embarrassment pulsed through me. Had anyone ever witnessed me being more pathetic? "Believe me, I can *never* face him again. Besides, he's back together with his ex-girlfriend."

"That's too bad," she said. "He sounded like a nice guy."

"I guess," I said, shrugging. "It's no big deal."

My mom sat back in her chair. "Honey, I know I was pretty down on love for a while, and I'm sorry about that." She reached over and took my hands in hers. "I don't want you to think there's something wrong with being all ga-ga over a boy." When she said "ga-ga," she opened her eyes wide and did a weird little dance with her head. "It's a wonderful feeling."

"Yeah," I said. "Sure it is." I gently extracted my hands from hers and stood up. It seemed to me that the

251

only thing worse than my mom gushing over being in love with her new boyfriend was my mom gushing over love *in general*. To avoid any further conversation on the subject, I told her to relax while I took care of the dishes.

It was a small price to pay.

♥ ♥ ♥

Seniors don't work on the "Last Will and Testament" issue of the *Spectator*—they're not even supposed to *see* it, since it's meant to be all hush-hush until graduation. So it was surprising when Max came by the office late Thursday, just as I was turning off the computers.

"Hey," he said.

"Hey," I said. I hadn't seen him since our fight in the cafeteria. Funnily enough, I hadn't really thought about him since then, either.

"I was hoping you'd be here," he said. "I wanted to let you know that my meeting with Mr. Michaels was great—he told me the administration's really happy about the article and everything. Good news, huh?" He was palpably relieved, and I realized Todd's accusation had been dead-on—Max really *had* been worried about being valedictorian.

I flipped off the last computer. "I guess," I said. How had I not known that about him? How had I not seen that he was the kind of person who would put his own needs above the needs of the paper?

"I owe you an apology," he said. "I shouldn't have thought that stuff about you." He looked straight at me. "I'm really sorry."

"Oh," I said. "Well . . . thanks." I grabbed my jacket and bag from Mr. Barton's desk.

"Hey," he said, bouncing up and down a little on his toes. "I left you something in my last will and testament." He held a piece of paper in my direction. I took it from him and skimmed down the page, purposely skipping the words that followed Anya's name. "You left me the *Spectator*," I said. "And your undying admiration for what a great reporter I am." I shook my head in amazement.

Max, misunderstanding my amazement, smiled at me. "Pretty cool, huh?"

I laughed in spite of myself. Did Max really think the *Spectator* was his to leave anybody? But all I said was, "Thanks, Max." I started for the door and Max held it open for me. As we made our way down the hall, I was reminded of all the times back when we'd been a couple that we'd walked out of the *Spectator* office together, traveling this hallway hand-in-hand or with our arms around each other.

But instead of feeling sad or nostalgic, all I felt was incredulous. Max didn't know the first thing about me.

And apparently I didn't know the first thing about him, either. He'd thought I was scheming and vindictive. I'd thought he was a daring rebel.

We weren't soul mates; we were strangers.

"So," he said as we stepped outside into the soft spring twilight. "You want to get some coffee or something?"

I guess I could have tried to figure out what he meant by that offer. Did he want us to be friends? Did he want to make amends for being such a jerk about the article? Did he just want my company? But instead of thinking up my own questions, I thought about his.

You want to get some coffee?

The answer was so obvious I didn't even have to think about it. "No thanks," I said. Then I gave him a little wave and walked over to my car.

♥ ♥ ♥

The night of my celebratory dinner, I was running totally late since I couldn't find the one pair of sandals I have that don't kill my feet. Clara, my official date, had arrived punctually, and now she was downstairs, rattling her car keys and yelling for me to hurry up.

I crawled into the back of my closet on my hands and knees, sure that somewhere in there was the box with my sandals. I found a pair of ancient Skechers I hadn't worn since eighth grade, three empty shoe boxes, and one box that I didn't even bother to open since it was way too heavy to contain shoes that weren't made of lead. Finally, wedged under an ancient pair of ski boots, I found the sandals. Crawling out of the closet with them clutched triumphantly in one hand, I bumped into something leaning against the wall. At first I thought it was my stupid middle-school diploma, which my mother had inexplicably insisted on having framed, but then I realized it was the *New York Times* profile Max had given me for my birthday.

Still holding the sandals, I pulled the framed profile out of the closet and started reading it, laughing at the part where I was quoted as saying, "All happy world leaders are alike; each unhappy world leader is unhappy in his own way." It really was a funny piece of writing. I remembered how happy I'd been when he gave it to me, but remembering that didn't make me unhappy. It was actually kind of cool. Someone had once liked me enough to make me something that great.

I was so busy reading, I didn't notice Clara had come into the room until she said, "Okay, you're not going to start freaking out about Max now, right?"

I shook my head. "Not a bit," I said. I realized that the heavy shoe box in the closet must have been the one I'd filled with the CDs he'd given me.

As if she could read my mind, Clara said, "We're not going to have to start listening to Wilco again, are we?"

I laughed. "They're not a bad band," I said.

"Whatever," said Clara, going over to my CD player. "You realize we're going to be, like, way late to this party of yours."

As I finished reading the profile, the opening notes of "Dancing Queen" filled the room. I turned to see Clara grinning at me. She cranked the volume as loud as it would go, swaying back and forth and singing into an imaginary microphone.

I knew we were going to be late to the party, but I didn't care. I lifted my arms over my head and started swinging my hips. It had been ages since Clara and I danced to ABBA.

And then I realized something.

"This is the ninth commandment!" I shouted.

"What?" Clara shouted back.

"'Embracing change,'" I said. "I'm over Max."

Clara shook her head, laughing. "I can't hear you," she yelled, and I laughed, too, not bothering to repeat myself.

Clara and I danced all the way to the end of the song. And when it ended and the next one came on, we just kept dancing.

PART THREE
The Beginning
♥ ♥

· · · · ·

THE FIRST DAY OF MY INTERNSHIP was warm and
sunny but not hot, one of those perfect June days
that make you forget how by July you're going to wish
you lived in Antarctica. As I walked across town from
Grand Central, I saw I wasn't the only one enjoying the
weather—when New Yorkers are strolling along, not in
a rush, smiling randomly at strangers, you know it's
truly a beautiful day.

The day before had been graduation. I'd listened to
Max's valedictorian speech, and it was like watching a
show you used to love when you were in junior high. You
remember thinking it was hilarious and deep, but now
it's just kind of boring. Then Clara and I went over to
Martha's and helped her get ready for the prom, and I
kind of had the same feeling. I was happy for Martha

because *she* was so happy, but it wasn't the way I'd felt when she was falling in love with Todd and I was still in love with Max. I *knew* what she felt, but I didn't *feel* what she felt.

If love was a disease, I'd been cured.

♥ ♥ ♥

As I showed the guard the security pass that had come in the mail, the confidence I'd had strutting across town started to evaporate. I was about to walk into a room full of strangers. What if all the other kids were losers? What if all the other kids were cool, as in too cool for me? What if we got a lunch break and nobody wanted to have lunch with me? I made a mental note to text my dad if we were going to have a lunch hour. Maybe he'd be free to meet me so I wouldn't have to sit by myself at Au Bon Pain like a leper.

There were about twenty kids already in conference room three. I was glad to see that everyone looked as uneasy as I felt. People were darting glances at each other, trying to check everyone out without being obvious about it. There was a buffet set up at one end of the room; a few people were standing around it, but I was too nervous to eat.

Chairs were set up in two rows around a big table. Most people were sitting by themselves with at least one empty chair on either side of them. I grabbed a seat in the outer ring at one end of the table, and then I just sat there, feeling totally irritated with myself for not having brought a book to read. The girl two seats down from me was reading the *Times*, which, if you ask me, was kind of kiss-ass. Or was it? Maybe *I* should have been reading the *Times*. There was a stack of them sitting in the middle of the table, and just as I'd decided to get one, the door opened and three people, two men and a woman, came into the room.

"Good morning," said the one of the men. Except for his being clean shaven, he looked a little like Mr. Barton. The other guy was way older, with white hair, while the woman looked as if she might have graduated from college recently.

"Did everyone get enough to eat? We have loads of stuff." She pointed to the table where two of the interns were still standing. One had his back to the conference table and was pouring a cup of coffee, the other was facing us, eating a doughnut.

I looked at the guy who was pouring the coffee. He was wearing a pale yellow oxford, and something about the way his hair hit his collar looked familiar. I'd seen the back of that head before. But—

I realized who it was just as he turned around, and my heart started to race. God, he was cute. For a split econd, I let myself remember what it felt like to have his arms around me, how great a kisser he was. Then I remembered how our kiss had *ended*, and I cringed. As his eyes scanned the room for an accessible empty chair, I tried to make myself as small as possible in my seat, but when I stupidly glanced up to see if he'd sat down yet, we made eye contact. He raised an eyebrow, and the next thing I knew, he was making his way over to where I was sitting.

"Hi," he whispered, taking the seat next to mine.

"Hi," I whispered back. Why hadn't I at least answered his e-mail? I could have just shot back something completely banal, like, *Sorry to have freaked out on you, thanks for a mostly fun time.* I could have written *anything*. Anything would have been better than trying to pretend (like a total idiot) that the whole night hadn't happened.

"Welcome to *The New York Times*," said the older man. "We're thrilled to see so many bright young people interested in journalism."

I couldn't concentrate on a word he said. Gene leaned forward and put his bag on the ground, and as he did, his sleeve slid up his forearm, which was tan and covered in soft, blond hair. Blushing, I turned away, hoping that staring at the man who was talking would make it possible for me to think about something other than the cute guy who'd gotten back together with his ex-girlfriend right after having the worst date in the history of the world with yours truly.

Suddenly I felt something poke me in the side. I looked down at the single word Gene had written on the pad of paper he was holding.

SO.

I took the notebook, trying to think of a response cool enough to obliterate my psycho behavior back in April. But even if one existed (which I highly doubt), my shaking hand would never manage to pen it. I settled for brevity.

SO,

I wrote back. The woman said something (I had no idea what) about journalistic integrity.

A minute later, I felt another poke. Smiling, I looked down to see what he'd written. SO . . . THE LAST TIME I SAW YOU, YOU WERE PRETTY HUNG UP ON THAT GUY.

I thought for a second, then wrote, how's the heiress? I heard you reconciled.

He read what I'd written, then bent over the notebook and wrote furiously before passing it back. YOUR SOURCES WERE VERY MISINFORMED.

He'd underlined "very" about ten times.

A wave of excitement passed over me, but it wasn't because of the woman's observation that ". . . the power of the press must be wielded responsibly. . . ."

I'm glad,

I wrote, returning the notebook without looking at him. A second later, it was back on my lap.

REALLY?

My heart was pounding. I forced myself to look at him.

"Yes," I said. I didn't realize I'd said it out loud until I heard the silence in the room.

"Sorry, did somebody say something?" asked the woman.

I sank low in my chair, wishing I could disappear. Gene's face was red with the effort he was putting into not laughing.

"Anyway," continued the woman, "what we're hoping you'll take from this summer is twofold . . ."

Still looking at me, Gene took the notebook off my lap. As he wrote I noticed his eyes were light brown with specks of green, and when he finished, I had to force myself to stop looking into them and read what he'd written. We'd been staring at each other so intently I was sure his writing would be illegible, but when I dropped my eyes from his to the note, I could read it easily.

COFFEE LATER?

My heart flipped over as I read and reread his invitation. I wanted to grab the pen from his hand and write *YES!!! YES!!! YES!!!*

But I stopped myself. Because what if I *did* write *Yes*? Would Gene and I get together? Would we *stay* together? Or would my nightmare scenario—the one in which he drives me home and then says, "I think we should just be friends"—come true?

I mean, look at where having a boyfriend had gotten me last time. It was enough to make me write *No*. Why take the risk? Surely someday somebody would invent a crystal ball to tell you whether or not a relationship would work out *before* it started. When that happened, I could start dating again.

But by then, Gene would be long gone. And I didn't want Gene to be long gone.

Which meant risking a one-way ticket to *Breakup Bible* City.

I closed my eyes for a second and inhaled slowly, remembering how much heartache sucked. Then I put pen to paper and wrote my answer to Gene's question.

He read the three letters I'd written, and his face broke out in a huge smile. He was still smiling as he flipped his notebook shut and put it back in his bag.

And as the woman described the important role a free press plays in a democratic society, I realized I was smiling, too.

ACKNOWLEDGMENTS

This book was made possible by generous grants (in the form of time, energy, and solutions to the most seemingly intractable problems) from the Gantcher family—Benjamin, Julie, Neal, and Rebecca. And by Saint Ann's. Of course.

MELISSA KANTOR is the author of the best-selling *Confessions of a Not It Girl* and *If I Have a Wicked Stepmother, Where's My Prince?* (a 2006 American Library Association Teens' Top Ten). She is a teacher in Brooklyn, New York, where she lives with her husband, the poet Benjamin Gantcher, and their son. Visit her at www.melissakantor.com